HER SINFUL ANGEL

HER ANGEL: ETERNAL WARRIORS
BOOK 5

FELICITY HEATON

THE HER ANGEL WORLD

HER ANGEL: BOUND WARRIORS

Book 1: Dark Angel

Book 2: Fallen Angel

Book 3: Warrior Angel

Book 4: Bound Angel

HER ANGEL: ETERNAL WARRIORS

Book 1: Her Guardian Angel

Book 2: Her Demonic Angel

Book 3: Her Wicked Angel

Book 4: Her Avenging Angel

Book 5: Her Sinful Angel

Discover more available paranormal romance books at:
http://www.felicityheaton.com

Or sign up to my mailing list to receive a FREE vampire romance ebook, learn about new titles, be eligible for special subscriber-only giveaways, and read exclusive content including short stories:
http://ml.felicityheaton.com/mailinglist

CHAPTER 1

It had started out like any other day in his kingdom.

He had risen at seven sharp, based on Greenwich Mean Time, and had crossed the black stone floor of his expansive bedroom to his equally as impressive bathroom. There he had showered and carefully attended to his grooming. With a black towel slung low around his hips, he had ventured into his wardrobe to select one of the black tailored suits that hung from numerous rails.

It had gone downhill from there.

As always.

He had found the suit he had desired to wear, only to discover a crease pressed into the finely woven wool fabric.

That had led to the first death of the day.

The impudent fallen angel who had been responsible for ensuring his wardrobe was perfect had been sent back to Heaven.

With his wings missing.

And in pieces.

The last part wasn't his fault. The idiot should have remembered to teleport before hitting the pavement of the courtyard far below the black fortress in the bottomless pit of Hell.

Of course, it might have helped if he had allowed the maggot to retain his ability to teleport.

Lucifer smiled grimly to himself and flicked a speck of dust off the right sleeve of his newly-pressed suit, his golden eyes fixed on the black cragged lands beyond the window of his study.

Breakfast had been a rather sober affair this morning. His attendants were on edge around him today, more than they usually were anyway. He couldn't think why. Perhaps it had something to do with the fact that they had narrowly avoided being hit by the falling angel when they had been crossing the courtyard.

A chuckle slipped from his lips as a replay of the event played across his mind.

By now, all of Hell would know he was not in a good mood.

He had planned to improve it by heading out to the distant plateau where Heaven had stationed a group of angels and use the power of his voice to see if he could sway a weak one into falling. There was a space in his ranks that needed filling, and corrupting angels always brightened the dreariest of days.

A pale orange glow lit the wall of black rock beneath the plateau, adding a dash of colour.

He despised that band of gold.

The lava river encircled his fortress and marked a boundary that by law he couldn't cross, not until the time between his scheduled battles with Apollyon, an angel who had served Heaven for centuries before turning his back on that realm for the sake of a woman, had passed.

Lucifer hadn't won one in centuries. He had taken several for the team without receiving any shred of gratitude in return, allowing the angel to defeat him so he would remain trapped in the bottomless pit and a band of fallen angels bent on destroying the mortal world would remain caged here with him.

Of course, it might have helped if he had informed Apollyon that he was losing on purpose, but storing up his losses and waiting for the perfect opportunity to mention to the angel what he had been doing all these millennia had been too enticing to resist.

His smile stretched a little wider.

It had been most satisfying to reveal to the angel just a few weeks ago that his hard won victories had been hollow and see the look on the bastard's face.

The momentary flicker of pleasure that shot through his veins dimmed as he lowered his gaze back to the courtyard and it fixed on the current thorn in his side.

There was no chance of improving his mood now. It had hit rock bottom, thanks to a certain angel of Heaven.

Mihail.

When he discovered who had awoken the angel to his true purpose, restoring his memories at the same time, he would send his finest legion to Heaven to destroy them.

The angel flicked his long white hair over his shoulder but kept his icy blue eyes locked on Lucifer. The silent challenge they issued didn't go unnoticed, but Lucifer knew better than to rise to it. Mihail couldn't enter his fortress, thanks to powerful wards Lucifer had put in place after their last battle.

A fight that had seen almost half of Hell destroyed and turned to rubble.

Lucifer had enjoyed the millennia of peace that had come afterwards. Battling Apollyon was merely a workout for him, but fighting Mihail was a war and one that could easily claim his life. Only Mihail held the power to truly defeat him. Apollyon could only wound him.

Mihail could kill him.

Lucifer had no interest in dying and being thrust into limbo, wandering eternity as nothing more than a soul, maddened by being caged in a bleak world where he couldn't communicate with those around him and tormented by his sins.

Not until he had settled a score with his former master and had his vengeance.

Not even then.

He never wanted to go to that dark place few angels knew existed.

Those who didn't know of it had no fear of death, trusting they would be reborn in Heaven upon their demise, restored to their former glory, albeit without memories of their previous life.

The fools.

Lucifer knew better.

He had seen the corrupted souls of angels in the far reaches of his realm, heard their whispers on the wind and felt their suffering in his blood.

True death was possible for any angel.

He knew because he had killed one on occasion, damning them to a hellish existence.

Lucifer would damn Mihail in the same manner without even flinching if he had the chance.

The white-haired angel moved a step closer, his enormous glossy white wings shifting with the action, stark against the black pavement of the semi-circular courtyard and the obsidian armour he wore. The patches of golden skin visible between the black greaves that encased his shins, the strips of black that protected his hips, his short black breastplate and his vambraces that shielded his forearms bore tattoos now when once they had been clean and pure.

Lucifer's smile returned.

Mostly because he felt sure that the bastard angel despised those tattoos and the one who had put them there—the fallen angel this male was linked to through duty and powers.

If Lucifer had the power, he would gift those angels who were linked to Mihail and his brethren with the ability to do more than merely change their skin by adding ink that would also appear on their counterpart. He would give them the power to amend their appearance in other ways. He wasn't talking about haircuts and piercings.

He was talking about wounds.

Mihail spread his white wings, regaining Lucifer's attention, but not for long. It drifted away again, his gaze roaming downwards and across the courtyard, to the prone mortal that lay like an offering on an altar between his fortress and the angel.

A woman.

Lucifer's golden gaze narrowed on her and questions filled his mind again, ones that wouldn't be ignored this time. Why had Mihail dumped an unconscious female in his courtyard?

Was she bait?

If the male thought he would leave the safety of his fortress for the sake of a mere mortal female, the fool was mistaken.

He eyed the female in question.

She had hair the colour of autumn leaves threaded with gold, strewn like the river of lava he so despised across the obsidian flagstones. Her skin was pale beneath the black dust that spotted it and the tear across the stomach of her white blouse. The thin shirt gaped open at the collar, and the angle of her body, with her shoulders flat against the paving and her arms resting above her head, caused the curve of one breast to show together with a hint of cream lace.

She looked weak like that.

Vulnerable.

Submissive.

Lucifer canted his head and allowed his gaze to drift over her. Her hips lay rotated, her left one raised and her knee pressing against the flagstones, pointed towards him. The short black skirt she wore rode high on that leg, revealing a long rip in her stockings.

What had Mihail done to the female before laying her out like a virgin sacrifice in his courtyard?

Lucifer growled low in his throat, the urge to leave his fortress and beat an answer out of the angel racing through his blood, setting it on fire. He had no love for mortals, and no use for females of their race when he had given up attempting to sire another child, but the sight of the woman stirred darkness in his veins, a deep and commanding need that he couldn't quite decipher.

The angel backed off a step, his pale blue eyes still locked on Lucifer.

He was up to something. Playing the snake to his Adam, and she was the forbidden fruit. Lucifer wouldn't be tempted though. He was stronger than the angel believed. More cunning.

Two of his angels flew over the tall spires of black rock that surrounded the courtyard and fortress, their crimson wings urgently beating the hot air as their scarlet eyes scoured the flagstones. Mihail turned to face them and the angels broke apart, keeping their distance from the male. They followed the curve of the wall towards the fortress and landed close to it, their wings furling against their red-edged obsidian armour as they touched down.

The larger of the two males rolled his shoulders and stomped forwards, cautiously approaching the female.

The other drew a long curved black blade from the air and set his sights on Mihail, snarling at him through twin rows of sharp teeth.

The angel of Heaven backed off a few steps before turning away and taking flight, heading back over the spires of rock towards the plateau.

Interesting.

Lucifer lowered his gaze back to his men. They warily approached the prone female. With good reason. He had ordered them to retrieve her and bring her to the entrance of his fortress. He hadn't told them why. He had only warned them not to test his temper. No doubt they thought just eyeing the woman would be enough to have him trussing them up for punishment.

The larger Hell's angel scooped the female up into his thickly-muscled arms and she rolled towards him, her cheek coming to rest against his hard breastplate.

A growl curled from Lucifer's lips, rumbling up from the pit of his soul. He frowned at the hot need that pumped through his veins, a visceral ache that demanded he go down and take the female from his man and punish the maggot for touching her.

He clenched his fists at his sides, grimaced as his short black claws bit into his palms, and sharply turned away from the window. The female was nothing. The only reason he was bringing her into his home was because he wanted answers. He wanted to know why Mihail had brought her to Hell. He wanted to find out whether she was a trap for him and she was in on the plan.

Lucifer strode from the study and banked right along the corridor. Beyond the end of the hallway, the entire fortress opened up into a cathedral-like room in the centre of his home. He stepped out onto the walkway that ran around the one hundred foot high space and headed down the floating black stone staircase that cut directly across the enormous room and connected the third

5

floor to the second one. Above him to his right, the steps to the fourth floor flowed upwards.

Warm light from the gilded bone chandeliers that hung from the underside of the staircases flooded the room and washed over him, giving more colour to his skin. He glanced down at his left hand, closed his eyes, and turned away from it and the memories of a time when his skin had been as golden as many of the angels who joined the ranks of his men on falling.

A time when he had flown carefree in the world of mortals and had lived to serve his purpose.

A time before he had realised what his true purpose was.

Lucifer ground his teeth, shoved those memories away, locking them back deep inside him where they belonged, and strode onwards, following the open-sided staircases as they criss-crossed the high room. Below him, the tall twin doors of the fortress opened and the heavy thud of boots echoed up to him. He glanced down at the two Hell's angels, issuing a silent command to halt and wait for him.

He would take their new guest from here.

Lucifer stepped down onto the polished black floor of the entrance hall and took swift strides across it, his Italian leather shoes clicking with each determined step. As he approached, the two angels bent their heads, and the larger one held the female out to him.

He reached for her and tensed as an unfamiliar sensation shot down his arms and pooled in the pit of his chest, stopping him from taking hold of her.

It took him a moment to name the emotion.

Apprehension.

Lucifer sneered at the feeling and crushed it out of existence. The mortal was weak. If she was in league with the angels, he would crush her out of existence too. There was no need to fear her. She was no threat to him. There wasn't even a need to fear Mihail.

He took the redhead from his man, cradling her with one arm behind her back and the other tucked under her knees, and turned away from the angels to head for the stairs. Once she was conscious, he would begin questioning her, and if she spoke a lie he would know it. If she wasn't in on Mihail's plan, then he would keep her alive. She would become bait for the angel. The male was sure to return to take her back from him sooner or later.

Lucifer didn't care which it was. He had infinite patience when it came to taking down an enemy, and Mihail's demise was long past due.

He took the first step and paused as he glanced down at his cargo. Soft pink lips parted as her head lolled away from his chest, her breath escaping her on a little sigh. Russet brown eyebrows puckered and then smoothed, and Lucifer canted his head.

The world around him fell into silence as he studied her face, caught up in wondering what she was dreaming.

She wasn't a threat to him.

She was nothing but a mere mortal.

A weak creature he could end with little more than a thought.

So why did the weight of her in his arms, the warmth of her body against his, and the scent of her curling around him all feel dangerous to him?

CHAPTER 2

Nina groaned and rolled onto her back, tossing her right arm above her head. Rather than the expected soft pillow, it struck something firmly padded. She loosed another muffled moan and frowned, the urge to open her sore eyes and see what she had hit dampened by the riot in her head. Sweat trickled between her breasts and soaked her back where it pressed into the hard whatever it was she was lying on.

Her couch?

She couldn't remember it being this uncomfortable.

But if it wasn't her couch, what was it?

More than that, where was she?

Her frown deepened as she tried to recall whether she had gone out after work with her small group of friends, had possibly had a little too much to drink, and had ended up on one of their couches.

She couldn't remember anything after leaving work for the evening.

A prickling sensation ran down her spine and over her limbs, and she pulled down a sharp breath. She had probably drunk a little too much. It had been a Friday night after all. It wouldn't be the first time she had taken things too far when attempting to unwind and forget her worries.

A scuffing sound sent another bolt of panic through her bones and she cracked her eyes open, an apology to whichever friend had taken her in balanced on her lips.

Those words fled her when her gaze settled straight on a tall elegantly dressed black-haired man who stood a few feet from her, staring down at her with eyes the colour of pure gold.

Incredible.

But also terrifying.

She didn't know this man.

Nina shoved herself up on the seat, her damp palms gripping the black velvet and giving her purchase. Every instinct she possessed said to flee, to make an excuse and run like hell, but her head turned violently and all she could do was bite out a moan from between clenched teeth and press her left hand to her forehead.

"You are unwell?" The deep lush male voice washed over her like a soothing balm, easing the pain in her skull and her fear at the same time.

He moved, the soft click of his heels alerting her that he was drawing closer. Her panic went into overdrive again and she scrambled backwards to place some distance between them, hit nothing where the rear of the couch should have been, and landed hard on a cold floor with her legs sticking up in the air.

She stared in surprise at her tights-clad feet and the dark ceiling beyond them, needing a moment to take in what had just happened.

The man appeared above her, his head canting and his golden eyes narrowing as he looked down at her. "Did you hurt yourself?"

Nina quickly shook her head and clutched at the hem of her black skirt, keeping it covering her thighs. She had already made a fool of herself. She didn't need to go adding flashing her knickers at this man to that. Besides, she still wasn't sure who he was, how she knew him, or where she was. A flash of panties might be seen as an invitation, and as handsome as this man was, she wasn't about to invite him between her legs, no matter how long it had been since she had slept with a guy.

She rolled onto her side and scrambled back onto her feet, practically leaping onto them to evade the hand he offered. He stared at his outstretched hand as she smoothed her skirt down, his left eyebrow quirking in a manner that looked a heck of a lot like irritation to her.

When he moved, she expected him to advance towards her.

He retreated instead, backing towards an unlit black marble fireplace against an equally black wall behind him and lowering his hand to his side at the same time.

Nina looked around her as something dawned on her.

Everything in the damned room was black.

Where the hell was she? Some sort of goth retreat?

"There is no need to panic. I do not mean you any harm. You were left in the courtyard of this house and were brought in to keep you safe."

Nina's gaze whipped back to the handsome man.

And hell, he *was* handsome. The sort of man that could have a horde of women swooning with little more than a smile, their knees buckling beneath them. She wasn't immune to his beauty. She wasn't sure any woman would be able to say that she was. If they did, they would be a liar.

He oozed wicked sensuality as he stared across the room at her, his golden eyes fixed with hawk-like intensity on hers and his soft lips tilted at the corners into a hint of a smile.

Nina shook her head to rid it of the dangerous thoughts piling up in it and focused on what the man had said.

"Keep me safe?" She frowned at that, another ripple of panic running through her as she tried to guess the answer to that question and feared what he would say.

He toyed with the left cuff of his black shirt and then smoothed the fine sleeve of his black suit jacket over it, carefully adjusting it until it was perfect.

Just like him.

Nina shoved that little voice out of her head, determined to focus on the matter at hand and not the man at hand. She was in a strange place, in a stranger's house, and he was saying that she was in danger.

"You are safe now," he said with silken persuasiveness that had her dumbly nodding in agreement even when she didn't honestly feel safe. "The man who brought you here is gone."

"A man?" Nina's eyes widened as she tried to remember what had happened to her but her mind remained blank, refusing to supply anything beyond leaving work for the evening.

He nodded and smiled, and it hit her hard in the chest, knocking the wind from her and sending her head spinning.

Her panic returned full force. "I want to go home."

The man's smile held. "I am afraid that is not possible yet, but arrangements will be made for your return. If you tell me where you live, I will pass on the information and they will see to it."

They? Pass on the information? Was he the master of this house or a servant?

"London... I live in London. Anywhere in London will do." She figured it couldn't hurt to tell him the city she was from, but she wasn't about to hand out her address to him. She still wasn't sure whether there was another man who had taken her, or whether it was an elaborate lie to throw her off his scent.

What if this man had been the one to take her?

She twisted her hand in her white blouse, tugging at the material, struggling to breathe as a weight pressed down on her chest and she fought the wave of panic that threatened to sweep her away. She had to focus.

Her gaze fell to his hands as he toyed with his cuff again, neatening it, and her eyebrows pinched together. He had black nails. Why did he have black nails? Everything about him screamed businessman or butler, but he had black painted nails. She stared at them, unable to drag her eyes away. They were a bit too polished and impeccable. Were they false nails?

Acrylic?

They distracted her and she lost herself in pondering what they were made from and why he had black nails. It was only when the sensation of his piercing gaze on her faded and he moved his hands behind his back that she snapped back to the room. What was wrong with her today?

She was normally quite focused, but she felt foggy, her mind all over the place and easily lured into concentrating on the smallest things when the bigger picture was demanding her attention. She was starting to get the impression that it wasn't purely panic altering her behaviour, and that only panicked her further.

"You should breathe." Those three softly spoken words had her lifting her gaze back to the man's sober face. The moment their eyes locked, her fear subsided again and the weight on her chest began to dissipate.

Nina breathed slowly but steadily, drawing each breath deep into her lungs.

"Can you recall what happened to you?" he said.

She lowered her eyes to her bare feet, her dark stockings not quite black enough to make them blend into the cool stone floor, and frowned as she searched for an answer to his question.

"I remember leaving work." Nina looked down at her blouse, at the gash in the soft white material, and wondered for what felt like the hundredth time what had happened between leaving work and waking in this strange room.

Her head ached, throbbing deeply as she struggled to capture the barest sliver of a memory, just one moment that might help her understand what had happened to her. When the ache became a stabbing pain that felt as if someone was pushing a hot needle through her brain, she pressed her hand to her forehead, screwed her eyes shut and grimaced.

A flash of a shadowy figure blasted across her mind.

A man.

Nina raised her chin and opened her eyes, staring across the room at the black-haired man. "You were right. There was a man... but I can't remember what he looked like."

She tried but her head hurt so much that her stomach turned, sickness brewing there as the pain intensified. What had the man done to her? Was it drugs? Was that why her brain was so fuzzy?

"Do you know of any reason why someone might want to harm you?" The man took a step towards her and fear clashed with panic again, welling up to stir the sickness in her belly and bring bile up her throat.

She backed off a few steps, shaking her head in denial even though her heart and head screamed that there might be. It was entirely possible that someone was out to hurt her, and that meant that everything the man said had happened, had happened.

Someone had grabbed her, drugged her, and this man or someone from this house had saved her.

Nina's back hit a wall and she gasped. The man's eyes narrowed on her and she looked away, afraid he would see the truth in her eyes. She didn't want him to get into trouble because of her, at least not any more than he already had.

Had he been the one to save her?

Her throat closed again as she thought about that, sure he must have fought the man off in order to help her. She squeezed her eyes shut and pressed her palms against the wall behind her, her fingertips clawing at the smooth surface as she tried to anchor herself in the swirling storm of her emotions.

"I want to leave." She managed to get the words out but they were quiet, lacking the force and conviction she had wanted to convey in them.

Because part of her didn't want to leave. Part of her feared what was waiting for her out there. If *he* had sent someone to take her once, he could send someone again. She had known him too long to believe he would just let her go. She should have been on her guard after rejecting him. She should have expected him to pursue her with the same aggressive intent as he had the time she had fallen in love with him.

Before he had crushed her.

The man's gaze bore into her, commanding her to open her eyes and look at him, to find the strength to say those words with more conviction so he would let her leave.

She had to protect him.

He didn't know what he had become involved in by helping her and she didn't want him to pay for his kindness.

Not as she had paid for hers so many times and in so many ways.

"I want to leave," Nina bit out the words, putting force into them this time.

It had zero effect on the man.

"I am not sure whether the one who brought you here is gone and it is dangerous for you to be out there right now. Once we are certain that it is safe for you, you will be returned to London." He sighed, the soft sound conveying a wealth of irritation. "It might help if you would tell me why someone wished to kidnap you."

Nina froze. Would. Not could. He was on to her. Somehow, he was aware that she knew why the man had grabbed her and what he had intended to do with her. The little voice said to tell him, but she bit down on her tongue to stop the words from leaving her lips. The less he knew, the better. She was keeping him safe by keeping things secret from him.

"I don't know why someone would want to do such a thing to me. I'm just an office clerk. I'm not important in any way and I don't have any enemies." Nina tipped her chin up and looked across the room at him.

His expression darkened, his irises turning a full shade richer, more amber than gold, as his lips flattened and his features hardened. He didn't believe her. Her heart beat a little quicker as she held his gaze, her hands shaking where they gripped the wall beside her hips.

"What happened?" she whispered, a trickle of fear running through her veins as he stared at her, suddenly looking like the sort of man that it wasn't wise to lie to or cross in any fashion.

Gone was the handsome and charming man who could win any woman with nothing more than a brief smile. In his place was one who looked more demon than angel. A devil made flesh and blood. A man who spoke to her on a visceral level, calling to her primal instincts.

A warrior who was the embodiment of masculinity.

One who answered her question with nothing more than a narrowing of his striking eyes.

"You made the man leave… you didn't just find me," she whispered breathlessly, suddenly aware that she was alone with him. The gap between them seemed to shrink and the air in the room felt too thin. Her head turned, her heart labouring as she fought the onslaught of sensation and emotion. "You drove him away so you could bring me to safety."

He dipped his head, a slow and steady movement that didn't seem adequate to acknowledge the magnitude of what he had done. Most of the men she knew would have beaten their chests while grinning at her, their male pride on show for all to see.

He would have acted in such a way.

But not this man.

This man was different.

13

He barely acknowledged what he had done, even though it was worthy of praise and gratitude.

"Thank you," she said and he turned away from her, fixing his gaze on a door far to the left of the room.

"I will find you something to wear and will see to it that you are given some water and something to eat. Perhaps it will make you feel better." He strode across the room and was gone before she could respond.

Air rushed back into her lungs and into the room.

It seemed larger without him in it and she couldn't stop herself from wandering around the luxurious yet gothic and grim room as her panic and fear began to subside. Her fingers danced over polished black wooden side tables, the soft velvet of the chaise longue and the couch that stood facing it across an ebony coffee table. She caressed the cool marble of the black fireplace, lingering a moment to press her hot cheeks to it and savouring the cold before the stone warmed.

Her eyes drifted back to the black door the man had exited through. He hadn't been the one she recalled, that one had long hair, but that didn't mean he wasn't involved. She had to keep her distance from him, no matter how fiercely she felt drawn to him.

She jumped as the door opened again and the man entered, carrying a silver tray on one upturned palm. The ease he did it with stirred her suspicion that he was a butler, a servant in this house, together with his practiced smile and the way he spoke to her.

"Did you ask someone to take me home?" Nina eyed him as he set the tray down on the coffee table and poured her a tall glass of icy water from a pitcher. "Can you get me out of here and take me home?"

He paused and looked up at her through long black lashes. "I cannot do that. I cannot leave this place."

A brief flicker of something suspiciously like sorrow crossed his handsome face before he forced a smile, set the glass jug down and straightened. He smoothed his jacket down over his trousers in a manner that only strengthened her belief that he was a servant. It had to be the reason he couldn't help her leave, and couldn't leave himself.

"How long have you been here?" Nina eyed the water, her parched throat and aching head screaming at her to gulp it down. It might be poisoned. Laced with a drug that would knock her out again.

The man sighed, poured a second glass of water, and lifted it to his lips. He took a mouthful from it and nodded towards the other glass, a clear gesture for her to do the same now that he had shown her that it wasn't poisoned. Nina shook her head.

The water might not contain the drug. It might lace the glass.

He offered his glass to her with a smile, one that held a little more warmth this time, humour that seemed sad to her somehow. "I would not trust me either."

Nina took the glass from him, her fingers brushing his as she wrapped them around the icy tumbler. Heat shot up her arm and she almost dropped the glass when he snatched his hand away. Had he felt it too?

She couldn't bring herself to look at him as he paced away from her. She stared at the tumbler, at the spot on the other side where his lips had pressed, leaving an imprint on the polished glass. Her stomach heated. Flipped. She crushed the ridiculous urge to turn the glass around and press her lips there too and drank a mouthful from it instead. The cool water was bliss as it ran over her tongue and down her throat, instantly soothing her. Heaven.

"How long have I been here?" His rich voice swirled around her as she took another few sips and she felt his eyes on her again, burning her with their intensity and stirring the heat in her veins.

Nina slowly lifted her gaze back to his face and paused with the glass at her lips, the ripple of heat in her veins becoming a flood of wildfire as she found him staring at her mouth. The dark abysses of his pupils devoured the gold of his irises before he pulled his eyes away from her lips and raised them to lock with hers.

"I have been here a very long time."

She stared at him as those words sank in. He didn't look much older than she was, maybe just a couple of years closer to forty. Had he been working here his entire life?

Had he grown up in this grim place?

It would explain the edge he had about him at times, the dark and cold side of him that made her nervous.

That made her feel he had secrets locked deep in his heart.

Secrets as painful as the ones in hers.

CHAPTER 3

Lucifer stood in his study in front of the middle of the three towering windows, his gaze fixed on the distant plateau. White light broke the darkness there, a sign that angels were travelling between his realm and the mortal one.

A world he hadn't set foot in for millennia.

His golden gaze slid off to his left and downwards, towards the room where he had left the mortal female.

Her world.

He clasped his hands behind his back and studied the black stone floor. His black suit jacket stretched tight across his chest as he breathed slowly but steadily, his mind churning over everything he had learned about the woman in his custody.

He still didn't know why Mihail had brought her to him, and he couldn't help thinking that it was a trap. It was possible that the woman had been given instructions, orders that were buried so deep in her mind that she wouldn't remember receiving them. Some angels possessed the power to manipulate weaker creatures in such a manner, and everything she had told him yesterday had made it clear that Mihail or another angel had tampered with her memories.

If she had been given orders, then he had to wait for the right event to trigger them before he could discover why Mihail had sent her.

Lucifer narrowed his gaze on the floor, his focus on the woman.

He didn't think she was anything other than mortal, but it was entirely possible he was wrong about that. Some species could masquerade as mortals. Shifters in particular. It had been a very long time since he had encountered one from that species, long enough that he might not recognise them.

She could be a witch too.

But she didn't feel powerful to him. Her strength was barely a drop in the ocean of his.

Was she using a spell to mask her power and muddle his ability to detect lies on her?

He shook his head at that.

She hadn't lied to him when he had asked whether she could remember what had happened to her, but she had lied when she had told him that she couldn't think of a reason why anyone would want to harm her or have her kidnapped. If she possessed the ability to conceal her lies, she would have hidden that one from him.

There had been a haunted edge to her bright peridot eyes as she had uttered that lie and a spike in her heart rate that had warned him that she had walked the same path as he had millennia ago—a path of pain and suffering.

Of betrayal.

A path he still walked now.

He didn't know what had happened to her, and he didn't want to know.

She wasn't here so he could learn about her. She was here so he could discover Mihail's plan and take the angel down once and for all.

Lucifer dragged his focus away from her and fixed it back on the plateau.

Mihail was up to something and he had to concentrate on discovering what that was.

His focus slipped, his acute senses drifting to pinpoint the woman again.

Who had betrayed her?

The first stirrings of anger warmed his heart, warning him to pull his thoughts away from not her but the betrayal she had suffered before it was too late and his mood degenerated.

All of Hell would suffer if it slipped his grasp and his temper flared, but even the knowledge of what he might do in a fit of rage wasn't enough to stop him treading the dark path of his memories to a place he had tried to forget.

A time when he had trusted someone and they had betrayed him.

A time when he had been given no choice and had been powerless to stop his fall.

Lucifer curled his hands into fists, his emerging black claws cutting into his palms. He glared at the plateau as another white streak of light appeared and growled through his short fangs, the desire to teleport there and tear into the angels almost overwhelming him and shattering his fragile hold on his control.

He wanted to rip their wings from them just as his had been torn from him.

He wanted them to suffer the torture that he had, the agony of being cast from their home, slung into a bottomless and dark pit where only endless pain awaited them.

He wanted them to know how it felt to do all that their master asked of them, to carry out every terrible act and horrific crime regardless of how it had made them feel, only to have that same master betray them.

Lucifer snarled and slammed his left fist into the black wall beside the window. The stone shattered under the blow but he didn't feel the pain that ricocheted up his arm. He felt only the burning rage that lived in his heart, the pain of a thousand times of having his wings torn from his back, a hundred thousand lashings that had peeled the flesh from his bones, and a million hours of wondering what he had done wrong.

Followed by a million more contemplating his revenge.

He hadn't realised it at the time he had served Heaven, a loyal dog for his master, but he had been set on the path towards his fall from the moment he had been created. It had all been part of a plan to create balance between the three realms.

His master had shaped him, giving him duties and missions with little information and stating that he trusted him to interpret the missions and carry out the duties therein without aid. Lucifer had felt he had owned a position of power, a place at his master's side, but in reality he had been given as little information as possible in order to drive him into committing sins.

He had wanted to please his master, and he had ended up breaking unknown rule after rule, committing sin after sin.

When he had felt something stirring inside him, a darkness that had been destroying the light, he had wanted to stop.

It was then that his master had dealt the final blow.

He had been exiled from Heaven and thrown into the pit.

At the time, the pit had been a place of nightmares, filled with vile creatures bent on destroying angels, drawn to their light by a ravenous hunger to extinguish it.

Centuries into his torture, Lucifer had realised the reason the pit had been created. It had been designed as a place of punishment for angels. That had given him false hope that he could escape the pit if he served his time.

He had survived the torture his captors had dealt, the abuse they had inflicted upon him, using him against his will. He had wallowed, tormented by every sin he had committed in his life serving his beloved master. He had writhed in agony as he had tried to fight and claw his way out of the darkness to stand on his feet again. He had wanted to repent so he would be welcomed back into the fold.

He had wanted to return home.

But it had become too much for him, and the darkness had been too strong.

After what had felt like an eternity of fighting, he had surrendered to it, allowing it to fill him and vanquish his softer feelings in order to end his suffering and stop the pain. His thoughts had turned from repenting to revenge.

When he had eventually seized control of the realm through brute and relentless force, he had ended up changing it without really thinking about what he had been doing.

He had hunted and destroyed most of the original inhabitants of Hell and sent the rest fleeing to the far corners of Hell, allowing the weaker breeds of demons to emerge from the shadows and take their place.

Demons who had worshipped him as their master.

Lucifer hadn't realised the power he possessed as the ruler of Hell until Heaven had chosen to create a new race of angels to serve it. He had tainted the soul of the first angel during its creation, a mere drop of darkness that had spread through it and corrupted it.

He had seen the extent of his power in that moment and he had embraced it.

He had thought of nothing but revenge since then. Every act he had undertaken had been done with the intent of dealing a blow to Heaven as they had dealt a blow to him. He had begun to grow an army, welcoming the fallen angels into his fold and giving them power so they could destroy any of the remaining demons who sought to punish them for their sins and could carry out his orders in the mortal realm. He had shaped the weaker demons and sent them forth to corrupt the humans. He had done it all to strike a blow that would shake Heaven to its foundations.

Wars had followed, a struggle for power that was endless and beautiful.

Lucifer smiled grimly at the pleasing memories as power coursed through him, darkness that bled from his skin like smoke and writhed as shadows around his arms.

He pulled his fist from the wall and turned his palm towards him, splaying his fingers as he watched the black ribbons fluttering around them.

He had lived shrouded in darkness. A king in his realm. He had passed millennia without feeling a thing.

No trace of light left inside him.

Until Erin.

The day he had learned of his daughter's existence, he had been filled with a new purpose.

A desire to use her to finally achieve his dream of bringing down Heaven.

And the day he had first set eyes on her, something else had happened to him, something he had been fighting to hide ever since.

A tiny spark of light burst to life in the dark cold pit of his soul.

Lucifer pressed his hand to his chest, the soft fabric of his black jacket, tie and shirt cushioning his palm. He curled his fingers, digging the tips into the material as he felt that light inside him, tormenting him, growing despite his attempts to squash it out of existence. It refused to die though, kept spreading tiny tendrils through him, reaching ever outwards and gaining ground against the inky dark.

As it grew, it restored parts of him that were better off dead, softer emotions that had no place existing inside him or in his realm. Emotions that were dangerous to possess in Hell. There were still creatures here drawn to the light in angels.

If his legions learned of the light waging war inside him, if the demons learned of it, a battle for his throne would erupt.

Every creature with power in his realm would seek his head.

He growled from between clenched teeth and vowed that none would ever know of it. He made sure that his men never witnessed his moments with his daughter and grandson, and those were the only times he felt powerless against the light, unable to contain and control it.

He would find a way to expel that light from his soul again, because he would do anything to protect his position. He might not have asked for his role in this realm, but it was his to play now and he had come to like his life in Hell. This realm was his home, his everything, and no one would take that from him.

His golden gaze dropped back to the floor.

No one.

Any threat to his throne would be dealt with.

Painfully.

He had given the mortal female time to become accustomed to her situation, but now that time was up.

Now he would use the small sliver of trust she felt towards him and her attraction to him to his advantage.

The trick Mihail had used on her to scrub her memories would be wearing off. While she wouldn't remember that she had been taken by an angel, she might remember if Mihail had said anything to her or taken her anywhere before bringing her to Lucifer's fortress.

And now that Mihail's power was fading, Lucifer could employ his own abilities to sift through her memories as she tried to recall the events that had brought her to him.

If he discovered that she wasn't in on Mihail's plan, he would set in motion his own one.

He would implant orders into her head, ones that Mihail would unwittingly trigger if he returned for her.

The little mortal would become the instrument of the angel's fall.

And Lucifer would be waiting for him with open arms.

CHAPTER 4

Nina paced the small apartment she had been moved to, wearing a groove in the polished stone floor. It was cold beneath her bare feet. She wasn't sure what had happened to her shoes, but thinking about where they might be was a distraction she didn't need, not when she was beginning to panic again.

She had tried to sleep, but had woken sharply, roused from her slumber by something she couldn't remember now. It had been important, she felt sure of that. A memory? She frowned at the floor, turned on her heel and paced back towards the large tapestry hanging on the black wall, ignoring the niggling voice that mentioned for the thousandth time that there were no windows in her room.

It felt like a cell.

The walls closed in on her and she screwed her eyes shut, breathed out slowly, and drew down a deep breath to calm herself. She had to maintain her focus. Whenever she managed to get her mind off her current situation and unimportant details like her missing shoes, she could catch a glimpse of the shadowy figure that lurked in her fragmented memories.

Her head ached and she paused mid-stride, pressing her hand against her forehead. Sweat dampened it. She was pushing herself too hard again, but she felt that if she just kept her focus for long enough, kept driving forwards and not relenting, that she might remember what had awoken her.

It felt important.

She wanted to have something she could tell the man when he returned.

She hadn't seen him since he had brought her to the room, given her a set of clothes that were still laid out over the back of the red velvet couch in front of the unlit fireplace to her right, and had left her alone with instructions to remain in the room.

She hadn't seen anyone.

Not in all the time she had been here.

The grim corridors of the insanely huge house had been empty as the man had led her through them. Every single one of them. She hadn't even heard a trace of life in the building, other than her escort, and he had been silent the entire walk between the room where she had come around to find him watching her and her new one.

Nina flopped onto the four-poster bed to her left, the dark red silk covers cushioning her fall, cool against her back and her arms as she stretched them out at her sides. She stared at the black ceiling and the crystal chandelier that hung in the centre of it, her mind wandering as her focus slipped.

To the man.

He hadn't mentioned his name.

Because he was a servant?

She had never met a servant before, so she wasn't sure what the protocol was for them, or whether she should have given him her name.

It wasn't as if he had asked, and she felt sure that if it had been important or he had wanted to know it, he would have asked her.

Nina sighed out her breath and sank deeper into the soft mattress, her head filling with a replay of the hours she had spent with him and in this building. Questions began to replace the images, her curiosity getting the better of her now that she was beginning to feel bolder.

She was going to ask him his name when he returned.

She was going to ask him where they were, because this house didn't look like the sort she would find in London. The ceiling slipped out of focus and she struggled to bring it back to sharpness again. It wasn't the first time it had happened, but it was happening less often as the ache behind her eyes gradually dulled and the fog in her mind lifted.

The shadowy figure had drugged her.

It was wearing off, but he had definitely drugged her.

That meant she could be anywhere. She might have been out for hours. Days.

Her throat closed, her heart beating harder against her ribs, and she tugged the soft blanket beneath her into her fists, clinging to it as she fought the wave of panic.

She breathed through it, slowly and steadily, methodically pushing all of the frightening thoughts out of her mind so she could find calm again. With calm came clarity, and she needed that right now. She needed a clear head so she could think.

She needed to figure out what had happened and whether she was safer out there, or in this building.

The handsome man flashed across her eyes, his half-smile making her belly flutter and knees weaken even when she was lying down.

Part of her didn't feel safe around him.

Not because he was a danger to her, like the other man and her ex-husband.

But because he was too alluring, and the pull she felt towards him was too strong. She couldn't fight it, even when she knew that she had to in order to protect herself. She had learned long ago not to trust men.

Especially the handsome and charismatic ones.

And her host was as charming as they got.

Nina pressed her right hand to her chest, feeling her heart beating rapidly against her palm. She needed to get control of herself and shove aside the attraction she felt towards the man, because giving in to it wasn't an option.

She wouldn't put herself through that hell again.

The door in the right corner of the far end of the room opened and she shot into a sitting position, her heart leaping into her throat as her gaze darted towards it.

The man stood there, dressed as impeccably as before in a fine black suit and polished leather shoes, with his dark hair swept back from his face. All that black made him look as pale as a ghost, his skin white and flawless. Only his amber eyes added a touch of colour that added life to him.

Fire.

That fiery gaze burned into her as his eyes came to settle on her, narrowing slightly so his long black lashes darkened his irises to burnished gold.

"You are awake," he said, his voice as smooth and deep as an ocean, lulling her as gently as waves.

With practiced precision, he carried a silver tray into the room and set it down on the black coffee table near the red couch.

Food.

Her stomach grumbled at the sight of it. Fruits, something that looked like a sponge cake, and chocolate. Her belly growled louder, her mouth watering as she thought about breaking off a piece of chocolate and popping it into her mouth. Beside the food on the tray stood an elegant silver teapot and a single fine china cup on a saucer, with a tiny pot of milk and a sugar bowl.

Nina stared at the offering, wondering if she would look rude if she ran across the room to stuff her face with the food.

The man arched an eyebrow at her and then at the tray. "I can ask for coffee if you prefer it."

She quickly shook her head. "Tea is fine. Perfect. I love tea."

And she was rambling. She didn't need to catch the amused look on his handsome face to know that.

She edged off the bed and walked as casually as she could towards the couch. He shifted aside when she neared him and she almost paused to look at him, part of her curious about why he always moved away from her whenever she approached him. Was he merely trying to make her feel more comfortable?

Or was there another reason he wanted to keep his distance from her?

The suspicious part of herself locked on to the latter, filling her head with theories about why he might want to avoid being near her. She shoved them away as she sat down on the red velvet couch and snapped off a square of dark chocolate. Her stomach rumbled as she brought it to her lips and she had to fight to keep her eyes open as she placed the piece on her tongue and chewed. Heaven.

Nina swallowed the chocolate, sank back into the couch and sighed.

The man's gaze on her intensified and she lazily lifted her eyes to meet his. He was closer now, standing at one end of the coffee table and staring down at her, his head cocked to one side.

She was about to ask whether he had never seen a woman blissing out on chocolate when he spoke.

"Tea?" He was crouching before she could respond and she couldn't help noticing how his black trousers pulled tight across his toned thighs and higher.

Nina dragged her gaze away from the bulge and fixed it on his hands, watching as he nimbly lifted the silver teapot in his left hand and pressed the fingers of his right to the lid as he tilted it, pouring a tall stream of golden liquid into the waiting white cup. Steam swirled from the hot liquid as it rose towards the brim. With an equal measure of care and perfection, he slowly righted the teapot and set it back down on the tray.

Golden eyes slid across to meet hers. "Milk?"

Nina nodded and he picked up the small china pot and began to pour, his gaze constantly on hers. She held her hand out when the tea was golden, not too pale nor too dark for her taste. When he reached for the sugar, she shook her head.

"Sweet enough as you are?" he said with a wide smile that made her heart thump ridiculously against her chest.

She opened her mouth to bat the comment away, but he rose to his feet, coming to tower over her. Something about him standing over her like that, the warmth draining from his eyes as his smile faded, set her on edge. She wrapped one arm around her waist and reached for her cup of tea with the other.

"I make you nervous." He backed off a step and then another, and she wanted to tell him that it wasn't him, but she couldn't bring herself to voice that lie.

He did make her nervous.

He made her nervous when he was close to her, when he was kind to her, when he asked her things about what had happened to her.

When he looked at her as she knew he was looking at her now when her gaze and focus was on picking up the tea he had poured for her.

She could feel the heat of his gaze on her, knew if she lifted hers to meet his that there would be a touch of hunger in his eyes, desire that she had spotted in them before and that left her feeling breathless. The room closed in on her and she struggled to breathe as she reached for the cup. Her fingers shook against the delicate handle and she closed her eyes to shut out the room and everything in it, hoping that it would help her steady her nerves.

It didn't.

She could still feel his eyes on her.

She pulled down another steadying breath and focused harder, pushing aside the fierce sensation of his eyes on her as she opened her own and settled them on the cup. She gripped the handle and lifted it away from the saucer, bringing it to her as she leaned back. Her hand remained steady this time and she managed a few sips of the hot tea. The comforting taste of it settled her nerves even further.

It might have helped that he stopped looking at her in that instant and moved off towards the fireplace.

Nina studied him as she sipped her tea, taking in the elegant line of his back and how his shoulders tapered but were broad. His black hair was shorn around the sides and back of his head, but left longer on top, groomed back away from his face. She grew bolder the longer he remained looking away from her. Her eyes drifted down the straight slope of his nose, took in the high contours of his cheekbones, and even the tempting soft curves of his lips. Ridiculously handsome.

She could almost believe he had been made to tempt women into sinning.

He exuded wickedness and sensuality, and she felt the full force of it as he turned his head towards her, his golden eyes locking with hers before she could glance away and holding her immobile.

"Is the tea to your liking?"

He may as well have asked whether she wanted to climb him like a tree and kiss the living daylights out of him, because her heart did a stupid fluttering thing in her chest and her belly heated in a way she hadn't experienced in a long time. Desire flared hot inside her, burning through her veins, and for a moment she wondered whether he had drugged the tea.

It would have been the perfect excuse, if not for the fact she had reacted to him in exactly the same way when she had awoken to him yesterday.

Nina blamed whatever drug the shadowy man had used on her. It obviously hadn't worn off as much as she had thought.

"What's your name?" She blurted the question and his left eyebrow arched, a flicker of surprise crossing his features. "If I have to stay here, I at least want to know where I am and who you are."

"Lucifer," he said it with such a deadpan expression that she didn't have the heart to ask whether he was joking and had just pulled a name out of his head that suited the dreary house around her.

"You must have loved your parents for that one."

His expression darkened. "I do not have parents."

That explained a lot, but also left her with a heck of a lot more questions. Had her previous assumption been correct and he had been raised in this house?

God help him if he had. The poor bastard. It was little wonder he was so pale and looked so cold and emotionless most of the time.

Except when he was looking at her.

Sure, he had looked at her with cold, cruel eyes from time to time, but there were those times when they held banked heat, desire that had shocked her the first time she had noticed it.

"Nina." She offered her free hand but he only looked at it, keeping his station near the fireplace opposite her, with the table neatly positioned between them.

Like a barrier.

Nina lowered her hand to her lap and his eyes followed it, his irises darkening once more as his pupils dilated.

There it was again. That heat that stirred the same in her, breaking through the hard emotionless cold that normally filled the space in her chest. Was it the same for him?

Or was she being ridiculous?

The heat inside her grew as he lifted his eyes, slowly tracking the length of her arm upwards and over her shoulder, and the hunger in them grew with each inch higher he roamed. He sucked her awareness to him, pulling it away

27

from the room until she was conscious of only him and how he was looking at her.

Of the way his golden eyes seemed to brighten as they lingered on her face and then fell to her lips.

Her breath came quicker, heart racing as she fought the effects of his eyes on her and tried to shake them off.

It was impossible.

She felt as if she had fallen under some sort of spell and he was the one casting it on her by merely looking at her as if she was beautiful and he couldn't go another second without crossing the room and touching her.

A flash of him doing just that filled her mind, a stolen moment in which his hand would catch her cheek and flutter downwards to her jaw to tease her head back so his lips could taste hers and steal her breath from her.

Every inch of her trembled in anticipation, aching for that even when it scared her a little.

She couldn't remember the last time a man had looked at her the way he was staring at her right now.

No.

She could.

And it was enough to throw a bucket of icy water on her libido and kill it.

Nina averted her gaze.

The spell shattered.

She felt it break, felt his eyes leave her as he shifted back a step, one that lacked confidence and felt uncertain to her. He lingered a moment, nothing more than a heartbeat, and then the sound of his shoes clicking on the cold stone floor broke the silence. The door slammed and she flinched, spilling her tea on the floor by her bare feet.

Nina sat there in silence, her eyes closed and her heart racing.

What the hell was she doing?

She placed the cup down on the tray and wrapped her arms around herself as she stared at the closed door.

Whatever had been happening, she wasn't alone in her reaction to it.

It had rattled Lucifer too.

And Nina had the feeling that was a rare thing.

CHAPTER 5

What the fuck was he doing?

Lucifer stormed down the hall, shadows streaming from his fingers as he snarled through his fangs, torn between seeking out something to take out his anger on and returning to the room where Nina waited for him.

He reached the towering vestibule of the fortress before stopping dead.

The floating staircases that connected the floors of his home blurred and his fingers relaxed, uncurling to hang limp.

Nina.

She had said her name was Nina.

He'd had many women as guests in his castle, but never once had he known their name. It felt dangerous. Intimate.

With nothing more than a single word, she had entranced him.

Enslaved him.

He had stood there staring at her, pondering her name and running it around his head, discovering it had a pleasing ring to it.

One he could imagine uttering at the height of pleasure, when he was lost in the heat of passion with her, entangled and entwined in his bed.

Another growl curled from his lips and he managed another step before stopping again, his feet refusing to cooperate.

Refusing to take him another inch further from her.

Nina.

Fuck, he had never thought anyone or anything could have power over him again, but it seemed that single innocent word and the female it belonged to had somehow mastered him.

He snarled and forced himself to take another step, increasing the distance between them and denying the pressing need to turn around and go back to the room where she waited. He wanted to watch her, study her, until the end of time. As dangerous as it was to admit it, she fascinated him.

No female before her had captivated him as she did.

No female had a perfect blend of light and darkness inside them as she did.

Both the light and the dark pulled him towards her and he was powerless to resist. His feet shifted, not forwards this time but back a step, bringing him closer to her again.

He cursed, spitting the vilest one imaginable in the demonic tongue, and the ground shook. The gilded bone chandeliers hanging from the staircases that cut across the enormous space in the vestibule trembled, causing the light to flicker and even fade in some places.

What the fuck was he doing?

Was this all part of Mihail's plan?

Had the bastard tracked down the most beautiful, pure yet tainted female on purpose?

The angel must have known that she would lure him to her, that the seed of darkness that lived within her, the pain that had left its mark on her soul, would be irresistible to him.

But Lucifer had slept with many females who had been tainted by darkness, and he had never felt a pull towards them. He had never desired them.

They had been a means to an end, a method of producing an heir, a vessel that he could use to leave Hell and wreak havoc on Heaven without risking releasing the princes from their prison.

Nina was so much more to that.

He pressed a hand to his chest, clawing at his suit jacket as a weight settled behind his ribs, an aching heaviness that he hadn't felt in a long time.

An emotion he had never wanted to feel again.

Loneliness.

Even a king could know loneliness and despair born of fear that he would forever be alone, and it was a bitter and cutting sort of loneliness. It was a loneliness experienced even when surrounded by those who served him. It was despair that ate away at him even when he wasn't aware of it.

And he had never been aware of it before now.

He had always believed himself happy here, in his kingdom, a ruler of all that he could see. An entire realm was under his command and every creature in it bowed to him. He had a million under his yoke, willing to die for him.

A million servants.

Not one equal.

How long had he felt this way? How long had this feeling been festering inside him like a disease, creating a rotten core?

Lucifer looked back over his shoulder, down the corridor towards Nina's room. How was it he felt as if she could cure him, could scrape out the parts that had gone bad and replace those that had wasted away inside him?

That tiny flicker of light in his soul mocked him with the answer.

Because he was feeling again.

Erin had been the catalyst, the one who had reawakened emotions in him, and he had tried to keep them under control and vanquish them. She had made him weak and he hadn't fought hard enough, and now he was paying for it. He was paying for allowing them to gain a foothold inside him once again.

He should have put an end to them when he had first become aware of them rather than letting them grow.

Lucifer laughed at that.

There were a great many things he should have done differently in his long life, and none of them he could change now. The past was for angels as it was for mortals, an indelible path that nothing could alter. He had come to terms with that a great many centuries ago, but it still didn't seem to stop him from dwelling on the mistakes he had made. As if mulling over them would fix them. It changed nothing. He could only move forwards, keep walking tall and keep fighting, and perhaps one day he would have the vengeance he desired and everything he had suffered, everything he had endured, would be worth it.

One day.

His lips curled into a wicked smile.

One day the entire world would tremble at his feet.

The ground shook beneath him, rattling the chandeliers again, the vibrations running up his legs as they grew stronger. Black shadows swirled from his fingertips and curled around his arms, and his shoulder blades itched, his wings desiring the freedom he rarely gave to them. He snarled as his mood blackened, pleasing thoughts of standing atop a mountain and seeing the puny mortals and the bastard angels quivering in fear as his legions decimated them running through his mind. The quake followed his mood, violently shaking the fortress, and he grinned as a crack forked across the floor of the hallway like a lightning bolt.

A shriek shattered the hold the darkness had on him.

The fortress settled and the shadows dissipated.

Nina.

Lucifer was striding along the corridor in her direction before he even realised he was moving, his swift steps carrying him back to her. The floor repaired itself beneath his feet, the crack sealing and returning the stone to how perfect it had been before his temper had slipped its leash.

He focused on himself and employed a power he hadn't used in millennia.

The ability to mask his presence, making him invisible to mortal eyes.

Fear flowed from ahead of him, rippling over him like a stream, and he almost cursed before he caught himself and told himself that he didn't care that he had frightened the mortal female.

The door to her room was open and for a moment he feared she would have left her sanctuary, but then he reached it and spotted her inside the spacious apartment. Relief swept through him, a curious emotion he hadn't experienced in a long time and didn't want to experience now. He didn't want to feel anything.

Yet he found himself standing on the threshold of her room feeling a myriad of emotions that tore him in a thousand directions, none of which he should have been contemplating. He should have been moving on now that he had seen she was well and unhurt. He should have been heading out to the prison to deal with his business there, using it to eradicate the feelings Nina stirred in him.

He shouldn't be transfixed by the sight of her as she stood near the red velvet couch, her hands tucked against her chest, clutching the silky white material and pulling it tight across her breasts.

He shouldn't be fascinated by how her heart settled as he stood there and her courage returned, bravery he had noticed in her when he had come to see her and bring her food, intending to question her again. She had been stronger, had radiated alluring confidence in his presence, and had even questioned him.

She had asked for his name.

No one had ever asked for his name before.

And he meant no one.

When he had served Heaven, all had known it. When he had been cast into Hell, none had cared about it. When he had risen to rule this realm, they had given him a new name. The Devil.

In all the millennia he had been alive, not a single soul had actually bothered to ask him for his name.

He cocked his head as he watched her moving around the room. Mortals were weak, but she had strength in her. It wasn't physical. She was as frail as all mortals in that respect. It was emotional, and he had no doubt that it had been born from the ashes of her past and her pain.

Lucifer leaned against the doorframe, folded his arms across his chest, and studied her, the world around them falling away as he sought answers to the questions that refused to leave his mind.

What had happened to her?

What was it about her that fascinated him?

He had never really taken the time to study mortal nuances, not in all the years he had walked among her kind. They had never interested him before, and they shouldn't interest him now.

Yet she fascinated him.

She carefully brought her tea cup to her lips, took a sip, and then lowered it again as she walked around the room. A drop of liquid remained on her lower lip, trembling there, luring his gaze to her mouth. He stared at it for long seconds, losing track of time, before he noticed something else.

A tiny streak of a pale silvery scar on her chin, close to the left corner of her lower lip.

The longer he stared at that little mark, the stronger his hunger to kiss that spot grew inside him, obliterating his awareness of anything but that scar and her lips. Fuck, he wanted to press a lingering kiss to that scar and breathe her in. He wanted to feel her tremble beneath his lips and sense the anticipation in her, the stirrings of desire and need, a hunger that only he could satisfy.

He wanted to take the bold and dangerous leap to kissing her.

He wanted her taste on his tongue, craved the feel of her under his hands as he clutched her to him, and hungered for the exquisite feel of her hands on him. He ached with a fierce need to feel her gripping him, her fingertips pressing into his bare flesh as she moaned his name and begged for more.

The feel of her gaze landing directly on him shattered his fantasy, dragging him back to the room.

He stared across the narrow distance to her, his heart pounding against his chest, his blood thundering with a need to surrender to his desire and act out that fantasy with her right now.

Because there was desire blazing hot in those peridot eyes that held his.

Hunger that matched the one raging out of control inside him.

A need that had broken his focus and had caused his mask to slip, revealing him to her as he had watched her, lost in a vivid fantasy about kissing her.

Fuck, he wanted her.

She wanted him too.

A dangerous proposition.

As much as he wanted to satisfy the raging hard-on pressing against his tailored black suit trousers, he couldn't allow it. He couldn't let her sway him.

He had to remember that she had been brought to him by one of his enemies and she was only here until either that enemy returned or he discovered the reason Mihail had left her in his courtyard.

Lucifer shut down his emotions one by one, roughly shoving them back down deep inside of him and locking them away. Her expression altered with each one he crushed and brought back under control, the desire in her eyes fading in time with his.

He wouldn't allow himself to feel anything around her.

He had to fight it, because for the first time in what felt like forever, he was feeling fear.

Fear that she would hurt him when he had vowed no one would ever hurt him again.

"What was that?" Nina's soft voice broke through the hold his rising anger at himself had on him and he lifted his gaze back to meet hers.

"A quake. They happen sometimes." They happened a lot, but she wouldn't be around long enough to realise that.

"An earthquake in London?" Her auburn eyebrows rose and an incredulous look filled her soft yellow-green eyes.

Lucifer smiled grimly. He had forgotten that the part of the mortal world she was from rarely had such natural disasters.

"We are not in London, and it was only a quake of sorts. They mine near here." It sounded like a reasonable explanation to him but Nina didn't look convinced.

He searched for another way of covering what had really happened. It was imperative that he kept her true location from her, as he did with all his mortal guests. He had learned long ago that the human mind was fragile and often had difficulty comprehending that Hell existed. Even those who did believe it ended up in a bad way. It seemed mortals were all coded to panic and go insane when faced with the fact they were in Hell.

Lucifer looked towards the wall between him and the world beyond his fortress. His world.

Personally, he couldn't see why mortals he brought here had minor coronaries on discovering they were in Hell. It wasn't as if he placed his guests in the prison near the pit with the other souls awaiting justice.

"How far from London are we... and when can I go home?" Nina set her cup down on the saucer on the table and didn't flinch away when he brought his gaze back to her.

She stood tall, her spine straight and chin tipped up. He was coming to admire that streak of courage in her, and that only made her more dangerous.

The sooner he discovered what Mihail had done to her, the better. He needed her gone.

"A long way. Arranging for your return is proving difficult, but it is in progress. I am sure you can return home soon." He stepped into the room and her eyes narrowed.

She folded her arms across her chest. "How soon? I'm sure the man who took me is gone now and I'll be safe at home."

She didn't believe that. He could see it in her eyes and hear it in her heart as it picked up pace. The scent of her fear swirled around him and he was on the verge of asking who scared her when he caught himself and forced his mind to remain on his business instead.

Eliminating Mihail, and possibly her if she was indeed bait and in on the plan.

He focused on her, holding her gaze and using a sliver of his power to keep her under his spell. Her gaze softened, her peridot eyes turning glassy as she stared across the short distance to him. Her arms unfurled, falling to rest limp at her sides, and her lips parted.

Mihail's power over her had faded completely.

Satisfied that he would be able to delve into her thoughts, Lucifer took another step into the room and closed the door behind him, careful to keep his eyes locked on hers the entire time, keeping her held in his thrall.

"Have you remembered anything about the man who abducted you?" He let the words slip slowly from his lips, infusing them with his power to turn mortals compliant and keep her calm.

A little frown flickered on her brow, briefly narrowing her eyes. Pain danced in them but he held it at a distance for her, keeping it at bay so she would only feel a mild discomfort as she fought to remember.

A shadow formed in her mind, gradually taking shape. One that he recognised. Mihail. Lucifer exerted a little more of his power, controlling her to a degree and making her latch onto that memory even though it hurt her. The shadow of Mihail grew clearer, but not enough to reveal his appearance to Nina. The angel had masked himself well. Never mind. Whether or not Nina could remember Mihail was unimportant. All that mattered was whether she could remember being given orders.

"Can you remember for me, Nina?" he whispered and her eyes widened, her body beginning to sway as she stared straight through him as if he wasn't there, caught in her memories.

She nodded.

Lucifer saw it unfurl in her mind, a thousand fragmented memories that streamed past him like ribbons on a breeze. He took in all that he could, seeing her leaving her place of work in the centre of London, her reach the Underground station, and then her bumping into the shadow Mihail. She stiffened as he captured that memory, a stifled cry leaving her lips.

"Shh," Lucifer murmured to her, easing her fear as her heart rate doubled.

When it had settled back to a regular rhythm and she was breathing easier, he pushed a little, forcing her to focus on Mihail in that moment.

The angel pressed his palm to her forehead and the memory cut out. The next one was of himself in the room where he had taken her after his men had brought her in from the courtyard.

Lucifer frowned.

Mihail hadn't implanted any order in her.

Lucifer had placed orders into enough mortal minds to know that it had to be done before manipulating their mind to render them unconscious and scrub the memory of him from them. It didn't work any other way.

So if she hadn't been sent to him with orders unknown to her, why was she here?

He carefully released his hold on her as he pondered that.

Nina began trembling, running her hands up and down her arms as if she was freezing, her teeth chattering as her eyes darted around her.

"I hate this place," she muttered and shook her head, causing the tangled strands of her fiery hair to sweep across her slender shoulders. "It's like a prison cell. No light. No windows. It's horrible."

She ran both hands up her arms and clutched her temples, clawing her hair back from her face as she stared at the floor by his feet, still shaking her head.

Perhaps he had been a little hard on her, pushing her too much in order to sift through her memories.

"I need to get out. I need air. I need to breathe." Her gaze leaped up to his face. "I have to get away from him."

Him.

Lucifer canted his head and studied her. The same him that he had detected in her memories before when she had lied to him? A male who wanted to harm her and who she believed was behind her abduction?

He needed to know.

He couldn't deny that need any longer.

"Does someone want to hurt you?" He practically growled the words and she froze, her skin paling and her eyes growing enormous.

Her reaction gave him the answer he desired, but it didn't prepare him for the wave of emotions that hit him when she spoke.

"He'll stop at nothing... I said no... but it won't stop him. He sent that man... I know it. He sent that man to take me back... but I won't go back. I won't go through that hell again." She narrowed her eyes on him and bared her teeth as she almost snarled. "He won't hurt me again."

Lucifer stared at her, empathy rocking him back on his heels as the strength of her words struck him, her obvious desire to protect herself from suffering at the hands of this male again striking a chord in him.

Deep in his heart.

"I need air," she whispered and clawed at her hair. "God, I need air."

Lucifer growled at her, his fangs flashing as he bared them and his eyes burned red briefly before he regained command of himself. She didn't seem to notice his reaction to the word she had so callously used in his presence and for the first time in a very long time he was thankful for something.

The last thing he needed was her seeing him as he truly was.

A monster in the guise of a man.

She would never understand.

No one did.

"Please... I need air... I can't stay in here. It's too confined... too dark..." Her eyes unfocused and he was by her side in an instant, catching her arm to keep her upright and steadying her as she wobbled on her feet.

He had been wrong. He hadn't pushed too hard. He had come close to breaking her. If he had realised the pain she held in her memories, the fear she had locked in her heart, the darkness that now consumed and terrified her, he would never have forced her to recall Mihail.

Lucifer paused and stared down at the delicate female he held by the arm.

What the fuck was she doing to him?

He wanted to cast her away, to let her fall in a heap on the floor and suffer, but he couldn't bring himself to do it, not when every fibre of his being said he had the power to end her pain.

He had the power to give her the air she needed, the light she craved, and the freedom she desired.

But it meant taking her to a place he hadn't ventured in a long time.

A place that only brought him pain.

CHAPTER 6

Nina gradually became aware of Lucifer where he stood right in front of her, so close that she could feel his breath on her face as she stared up at him, her hands still clutching the sides of her head. A head that felt foggy again and ached so fiercely that she was on the verge of asking him for some painkillers when he silenced her by slowly raising his hands towards hers.

He didn't hesitate or show any sign of emotion as he placed his hands over hers and carefully brought them away from her temples. His golden eyes remained impassive, unreadable even when she longed to decipher the feelings they were hiding from her, feelings she felt sure were there, locked deep inside him.

Her pain faded as she lost herself in those beautiful and striking eyes, her fear and her thoughts flittering away as she recalled how they had looked when she had caught him staring at her.

How fiercely they had burned with passion and need.

Desire that had filled her with an ache to feel his lips capturing hers and the firm press of his hands against her overheating flesh.

His pupils expanded a touch, a brief flash of hunger surfacing in his eyes before it disappeared again and he cast his gaze away from her. He released one of her hands but kept hold of the other as he stepped past her.

Nina frowned and turned with him, following him across the room. He paused in front of the massive worn tapestry that covered a large section of the wall opposite the one with the door and held his free hand out as if to touch the cloth and the dark threads that had been woven beautifully to depict a scene of war that included dragons and creatures straight out of a fantasy novel.

His hand hovered above the tapestry though, a bare inch from touching it.

What was he doing?

His eyes closed, his long black lashes coming to rest on his cheeks as he dipped his head and frowned. His mouth tightened.

Just as she was about to ask whether something was wrong, his eyes flicked open and he casually shifted the tall sash of material aside, revealing the black wall beneath.

And an arched door.

Nina raised an eyebrow at it and stepped forwards. Lucifer held his free arm out, blocking her path to the heavy-looking dark metal door. Several thick padlocks each larger than her fist secured the side of it closest to him. What was through the door?

The sensible part of her brain supplied that it was probably the route to a torture chamber or something infinitely worse than the room behind her that felt too much like a cell.

The curious part said to make him open the locks so she could see what was beyond such a heavily fortified door.

She didn't have to ask.

Lucifer clasped each padlock in turn and she couldn't believe her eyes as they opened for him. No key needed. Some sort of fingerprint recognition? The locks looked perfectly ordinary to her though. No sign of a pad on them that could read his prints. How was he opening them?

With each lock that clicked and opened, the anticipation built inside her and she found herself leaning towards the door, filled with an urgent need to see what was on the other side.

"You need space, and even I can understand such a desire," Lucifer whispered in a low silken tone that seemed to swirl around her, leaving her hazy and feeling light inside, as if she might float away, high from the sound of his voice alone. He glanced across at her and the touch of wariness in his golden gaze grounded her for a moment before his voice worked its magic on her again. "I will show you to a place where only you will be allowed."

She didn't understand how that was possible. Did he mean that he would stop anyone from venturing into the place he was about to show her?

Lucifer grasped the elegant black metal handle on the door and pulled. A rush of cold air swept past her, stirring her hair, but it carried the scent of a summer meadow. She stared ahead of her, expecting to see an incredible vista, but there was only darkness.

A tunnel.

She couldn't see the end either.

How was it possible that she had caught the scent of flowers in the air that had rushed into the room? She swore she had been able to feel the heat of the sun in the breeze too, even though it had been cold. It had carried the promise of sunshine and light, of nature and freedom.

Was she dreaming? The sense that she had stepped into some strange fantasy world only grew stronger as Lucifer marched forwards into the gently sloping tunnel, his left hand still grasping her right one.

"Mind your step," he murmured gruffly and cold danced over her skin again, a chill that she felt sure had been born of the iciness in his tone rather than the cool darkness of the tunnel.

She peered up at him, wanting to catch a glimpse of his face to see if his expression matched his tone and he was angry about something, but she couldn't see anything in the darkness.

How did he know where he was going? His steps were sure, radiating the confidence that hers lacked, and he never once bumped into the walls on either side of them in the narrow corridor.

The stone was freezing beneath her bare feet, damp and slippery. She skidded as she set her left foot down on a broad cobble and Lucifer's grip on her hand tightened, keeping her upright.

A soft glow pierced the darkness, illuminating the roughly carved walls. Her surroundings held her focus for all of a second before something both incredible and impossible stole her attention.

Her eyes locked onto Lucifer's right hand where he held it before him, his palm facing upwards.

Above it, suspended in the air, was a twisting orb of amber light.

She had to be dreaming. She just had to be. Everything before that she had felt was a fantasy suddenly looked normal, everyday run of the mill things. Lucifer's ability to open locks with only a touch of his hand. Perfectly ordinary. A door hidden behind a tapestry. Normal as anything. A mysterious black tunnel that looked endless but carried the scent of sunshine and flowers. Utterly sane.

The fact that Lucifer seemed able to conjure a ball of light?

Freaked her the fuck out.

Nina managed to force her eyes up to his face. The golden glow played across his stern features, highlighting the coldness of his eyes and the hard set of his jaw. She had seen enough men looking irritated to know that he was upset about something, and she felt certain that her episode back in the room was the reason behind it.

She tried to take her hand back but his grip on it tightened and he looked over his left shoulder at her, his hard features softening for a moment, a sliver of a second that she might have missed had she not been looking for it.

But she saw it and it was as if she had looked into a mirror.

She knew why he looked so grim. She knew because she wore that same look, felt the same as he did, whenever she did something that threatened to destroy the guards she had in place around her heart.

Her episode wasn't the reason he was cold and distant again, his emotions switched off and his barriers in place.

She was the reason.

He had taken hold of her hand and he was regretting it.

Yet he couldn't bring himself to release her either.

"It is not much further," he said in a low voice thick with tension and she relented, allowing him to keep hold of her hand as she wondered what had happened to him.

What had he lived through to make him so fiercely protective of himself?

Was it anything like the hell she had survived?

What she had gone through had shaped her even when she had tried not to let it affect her. It had made her cold towards others, forever keeping her distance from them and sometimes lashing out with cruel words to ensure they wouldn't get too close to her. She hated it whenever she hurt someone in order to protect herself, but she couldn't stop herself from doing it. The need to shield herself and stop herself from being hurt again was too strong.

Her gaze roamed Lucifer's face and her heart whispered that he was the same.

That was the reason she felt drawn to him so strongly. It was because they were the same.

She wanted to ask him about it, but the look on his face warned her not to push him right now, when he was already feeling vulnerable and was liable to lash out in order to force her to keep her distance from him. She knew the signals from her own behaviour. She had to give him time. Time that she needed too.

She needed the space he had mentioned, the break from the dreariness of the apartment and the fear that her ex-husband would find her.

Or send another man to come and take her from Lucifer.

Her fingers flexed against his hand, clutching it a little tighter, her need to feel his strength too powerful to deny. He responded by glancing down at their joined hands and, for a moment, she thought he would pull his away, but he tightened his hold instead, squeezing her hand in a way that felt both gentle and protective, as if he was being extremely careful with her.

She tore her gaze away from his face when he glanced back at her again, fixing her eyes on the glowing orb suspended above his right palm.

Magic.

It was the only explanation her mind could conjure.

Somehow, Lucifer was capable of magic. Not parlour tricks like the men on the television employed, but real magic.

She had spent her teen and early adult years lost in fantasy novels about incredible lands, powerful mages, and extraordinary creatures. She had dreamed about living in such a world to see what it would be like for herself. She had never actually believed it was all possible though.

The part of her mind that clung to logic said that it wasn't possible. She was merely seeing what she wanted to see, because she was caught up in a fantasy herself, brought about by whatever drug the man had given her to knock her out and the mysterious man holding her hand.

He was mysterious too.

He had secrets, ones that warned her to keep her distance from him in order to protect herself and her heart.

Ones that drew her to him at the same time, making her want to peel back the layers and learn more about him.

She wanted to know his deepest, darkest secrets and in return, she would share hers.

The light grew and she peered ahead of them. The glow from the orb bounced off a door at the end of the tunnel.

That orb suddenly disappeared, dropping them into darkness. Her hand jerked against Lucifer's, squeezing it so tightly that she feared she would hurt him, but she couldn't bring herself to loosen her grip.

"Bear the darkness but for a moment, Nina." Lucifer's voice curled around her in the pitch-black and she felt hazy from head to toe as her name fell from his lips.

If he could perform real magic, he was using it right now in his voice, luring her back under his spell until her fear of the darkness began to fade and she felt safe again, no longer vulnerable without her sight.

His hand slipping free of hers brought that fear right back though and she wrapped her arms around herself, suddenly cold to the bone as she waited, listening hard for a sign of him.

Metal ground against metal.

A clack echoed along the corridor.

A moment of silence.

Then the creak of rusty hinges scraped in her ears and bright light flooded the tunnel, blinding her. She flinched away from it, shielding her eyes with her right hand at the same time to protect them from the onslaught.

The scent of flowers and nature hit her hard, rushing past her on a warm breeze.

Lucifer made a low growling noise and bumped her as he backed away, leaving her in front of him. Nina squinted against the light and stepped forwards, drawn towards it and the world beyond the half-open door. She gripped the handle and pulled, eager to see what awaited her.

She was aware of Lucifer backing further into the tunnel as the door opened fully, but the vista that greeted her on the other side stole that awareness away from him.

"Go on ahead," Lucifer gruffly said and she didn't hesitate.

She stepped over the threshold of the tunnel, from the cold black stone and onto the soft green grass. The light washed over her and she basked in its warmth as it touched her and chased the chill from her skin. It heated her right down to her bones and she walked a few steps across the grass before stopping and tipping her head back, raising her face to the sun, her eyes closed. Bliss flowed through her and she sighed.

It was wonderful.

Nina pulled down a deep breath of crisp, fresh air into her lungs and exhaled it with a wide smile.

She stood there for what felt like minutes, stealing pleasure from the feel of the sun on her skin and the clean air in her lungs, and then slowly opened her eyes, no longer able to hold back her curiosity about the world that surrounded her.

It was beautiful.

A verdant valley right out of a fantasy novel.

Lush green hills rolled downwards from where she stood, leading to a river that twinkled as it snaked through the valley. On the other side of it, mountains rose up, covered in thick forest at their bases but capped with snow on top. The azure sky was impossibly rich, a breathtaking contrast against the rugged white peaks.

The range stretched for miles in both directions before giving way to green hills that poked out from the thick woods.

Below her on the hills, long meadow grass grew, spotted with colourful flowers, creating a beautiful barrier between her and the river.

Nina took everything in again, struggling to make herself believe it. The whole scene looked impossible. Like a dream. It didn't seem real.

Was it even possible for the sun to feel so hot on her skin and everything around her to be so green when snow covered the higher ground?

She had never seen anything like it.

Nina walked forwards, entranced by the valley, her fear falling away. Peace flowed through her, a calm that ran as deep as her bones and made her never want to leave. It was wonderful. Incredible. She felt liberated.

Free.

A laugh bubbled from her lips, her smile stretching wider as her eyes darted over everything again.

That laughter died when she turned back to Lucifer, expecting to find him standing in the valley with her, the same joy she felt inside her painted on his handsome face.

He stood in the tunnel, swathed in darkness, a sorrowful edge to his eyes.

"What are you waiting for?" Nina rushed out, her smile coming back to the fore as she held her hand out to him. "It's amazing. The sun is so warm. You have to feel it."

His sensual lips twitched but he didn't smile. He didn't speak. He raised his hand, holding her gaze the whole time, and held it out with his palm facing her.

His flesh compressed, as if he had placed his hand against glass and pushed.

Nina's smile faded again, a frown replacing it. She didn't understand. She moved back to him, the valley forgotten as she tried to comprehend what was happening. Her eyes searched his but they didn't give her the answers she desired. Was she trapped in this valley now, separated from him by a glass barrier?

Was that the reason he had said that only she would be allowed here?

That panicked her and she reached out to touch the glass.

A gasp escaped her when her hand pressed against his, nothing keeping them apart, and she snatched it back.

"I don't understand," she whispered and clutched her hand to her chest, frowning at him.

He looked down at his feet and then slowly lifted his gaze back to hers, the pain in them catching her breath in her throat and making her ache to reach out and pull him through the invisible barrier somehow.

"I told you," he said, his voice cold but edged with sorrow.

He looked beyond her, a brief glance that tore at her heart and had her reaching for him.

He stepped back, the darkness closing in around him as if embracing him, and shook his head.

"Only you can enter this place."

Nina stared at Lucifer, his words ringing in her mind. She looked over her shoulder at the beautiful valley and then back at him, and it struck her that he wanted to enter it. There was longing in his golden eyes, a need that seemed deep, as deep as her desire to have him explore this strange new world with her.

"Have you ever set foot in this place?" She held his gaze when his eyes dropped to her again.

He shook his head. "I cannot."

That wasn't the whole truth. She could see it in his eyes. He had been in this valley but now it was forbidden to him for some reason. She needed to know that reason, but she didn't want to hurt him, and she knew that pushing him to answer would pain him.

He was already suffering enough.

"But you come here?" Nina looked down at his feet, at his polished black leather shoes that blended perfectly with the dark stone of the tunnel, and then at her feet, cushioned by soft green grass. "You come here to look at it?"

She raised her head again and he lifted his gaze above hers, fixing it on the mountains behind her. The sorrow in his amber irises grew stronger and the sigh that slipped from his lips told her everything that he wouldn't. He did come to this place, and she couldn't imagine what torment it was for him to see it and not be able to step into the light.

He was in the shadows still, as if the sunlight refused to touch him. Another impossibility. The sun was at her back, directly behind her above the mountains. Its light should have reached into the tunnel, together with her shadow, but it didn't. It stopped dead at the threshold.

A threshold that was made of smooth black stone.

A wall. Made of huge blocks. She slowly took steps backwards as she tipped her head up, lifting her eyes to the astounding view before her. It wasn't only a wall with a door in it.

It was one side of an enormous black fortress.

It loomed over her, several hundred metres tall, topped with gigantic spiked towers. Not a single window penetrated the wall.

Impossible. That word rang in her head again. The logical part of her pushed forwards once more, stating that she was dreaming, because while the valley didn't seem quite real, this fortress had to be a figment of her imagination. There was no other explanation.

Such a place couldn't exist in reality.

She had been enamoured enough with fantasy stories to dream of living in castles, and had read books on the most famous ones in history, planning to visit them one day. She felt sure that if this place was real, she would have read about it. A castle the size of this one could hardly go unnoticed by the world.

"I have not visited this place in a long time." Lucifer's smooth, deep voice drew her gaze back down to him. It was on the tip of her tongue to ask him why when he spoke again. "Return when you are ready."

She went to nod but froze in place when Lucifer held his hand out and a wooden flaming torch appeared in it. He casually set it into a metal holder on the wall inside the tunnel, as if making things appear out of thin air was an everyday occurrence for him and nothing for her to worry about.

She stared dumbly at the torch, tempted to go into the tunnel to touch it and see if it was real. Maybe she was dreaming, because things were getting stranger by the second.

"There is no exit from the valley, so do not waste your time looking for one."

Nina frowned at that and saw it as an opportunity to test him and see whether he had been in it. "How do you know if you've never set foot in it?"

Lucifer turned his back to her and disappeared into the gloom of the tunnel.

His voice whispered from the darkness.

"Because I created it."

CHAPTER 7

Nina slowly turned her back to the tunnel and the fortress and stared out at the beautiful landscape before her.

Lucifer had created this place?

Who the heck was he?

He had powers that made her wonder whether she was losing her mind, but those small things seemed possible when faced with the thought that he might have the ability to create an entire valley.

She crouched and rubbed her fingers through the grass, crushing it slightly in the process and releasing the crisp fresh fragrance. It looked, felt and smelled real. She was sure that if she dared to place a blade of grass in her mouth that it would taste as she remembered it too.

Nina rose back onto her feet and began walking down the slope towards the longer meadow grass and the river. Her mind churned as she took light steps towards the glittering water, the strong sun keeping the chill off her skin and the earth warm beneath her feet.

When she reached the tall grass, she held her hands out at her sides, allowing the tips to tickle her palms. Her gaze remained locked ahead, her thoughts fixed behind her.

With Lucifer.

Why had he created this place if he couldn't set foot in it?

Why would someone torment themselves with such beauty and light when they lived trapped in such gloominess and darkness?

The tall grass gave way to a strip of pasture and she crossed it to the river, walking as if in a dream as she listened to the rush of water over the rocks. The warmth of the sun faded as she stepped into the shadows cast by the trees across the river from her. She sat on the shallow bank, pulled off her ruined tights, and stuffed them down the waist of her skirt, hooking them over it so she wouldn't lose them.

A gasp shot from her lips as she dipped her bare toes into the water.

It was freezing.

Nina steeled herself and slowly lowered her feet towards the icy water again. It seemed warmer this time and she allowed it to cover up to her ankles. She sat there on the bank and stared down into the rippling water, watching it rush over her toes. Pebbles lined the bottom of the crystal clear river, a multitude of colours, all of which seemed a little too rich to be real.

She tipped her head back and looked up at the bright azure sky.

Was this place real or fantasy?

She laughed at the thought that Lucifer might have created it. He must have been joking. The strength of the colours around her was probably down to the fact that she had been locked in a black hole for two days, starved of colour and light. Her eyes would adjust soon and the grass wouldn't look so green. The sky not so blue.

Her toes hurt beneath the cold water and she pulled them from it, wriggling them to get some blood back into them. She twisted on the bank, so her back was to the water and her feet stuck out into the light. The sun instantly warmed them and they began to lose their redness.

Nina looked up the hill to the fortress.

It looked even bigger from down by the river, towering over her, a stark and grim sight against the clear blue sky.

The thought of having to go back inside filled her with dread, a longing to remain out in the valley instead, surrounded by light and colour. Something countered the dread though, a sense that Lucifer was waiting for her in that bleak castle, and part of her didn't want to keep him waiting.

She didn't want him to be alone.

She had a suspicion that he wasn't a servant. He was the master of the house and he was alone in it. Maybe he had a few servants, but he clearly lacked companions, and he equally as clearly desired her company.

For the first time in a very long time, she wanted company too.

Nina pulled her focus away from the castle and its owner, and lumbered onto her feet. She walked the riverbank, following it towards the right side of the castle. There was a red arched bridge in the distance and she could just about make out a smooth path that led into the forest. Curiosity drew her towards it, over it, and into the woods.

The path led upwards and she followed it as it wound its way through the tall pine and oak trees. Her feet began to ache from walking but she kept moving forwards, exploring the dense forest and enjoying the freedom to move around.

In the distance, beyond another hill, the forest was darker.

She frowned and moved more quickly, striding with purpose towards it, wanting to see what obscured the light in that part of the woods. Her breath sawed from her lungs and sweat dotted her brow and trickled down her back. She swiped her arm across her forehead, pushed her wild auburn hair back from her face, and trudged onwards.

At the top of the hill, she ran straight into an invisible obstruction.

Nina stumbled back a step and pressed her hand to the wall of black. It cut through the trunks of several trees and stretched in both directions.

Lucifer had been right. There was no way out of the valley. Had he simply built a wall around it?

No. Half of the trees were missing, as if the barrier cut through them, and now that she was squinting, she could almost make out a shadowy empty land on the other side.

Cold crept through her veins, bringing with it a sense that something was staring back at her from that darkness, and she backed off, each step quicker than the last.

She didn't stop.

As soon as she was a few metres away from the shadows, she turned and hurried back along the path. Each step sent pain bolting up her legs from the sore soles of her feet, but she kept walking, almost jogging along the path. She wanted to reach the river again. The sensation of being watched grew stronger and she threw a glance over her shoulder, afraid that she would see something behind her.

Nothing.

Her eyes widened.

In fact, she hadn't seen any sign of life in the entire time she had been in the woods and the valley. There were no birds and no animals. No fish in the river.

She was alone here.

Her panic increased, her heart thundering against her ribs as she reached the river and ran across the arched wooden bridge.

The shadows gave way to sunlight, easing her fears.

The grass cushioned and cooled her feet, stealing away some of the pain.

Nina slowed and breathed hard, chastising herself for letting her solitude panic her. She switched to cursing herself when she realised where she had been running.

She hadn't been running towards the light.

She looked up at the castle ahead of her.

She had been running towards Lucifer.

As if he would protect her from the monsters in her mind.

Nina laughed aloud at that and shook her head. She had gone insane. It was the only reasonable explanation for everything.

Rather than heading back to the castle, she walked the curve of the hill towards the start of the long grass and sat down.

Lucifer had promised she would be safe here and she did feel safe. Her gaze slid back towards the bridge to the woods below her to her right and she shuddered before shoving away the fear that tried to claw its way back into her heart. She was alone in this place. No one could set foot in it but her.

It was just fear and fatigue playing tricks on her.

She leaned back and lay on the grass, her arms spread at her sides and her eyes on the sky above her. Pale fluffy white clouds scudded across the azure canvas, catching her focus. She followed them one by one, until she fell into a sort of trance, lazing in the sunshine and letting the world drift by as she relaxed.

The sense of peace returned and with it came the calm she needed. She embraced it this time, using it to keep all the questions at bay so she could steal all the pleasure she could from this moment.

Minutes ran into each other until she lost track of time and her thoughts turned back to Lucifer.

Did he own the castle? She wanted to believe that he lived there by choice, but she couldn't make herself swallow that lie.

He had said that he couldn't leave it, and she hadn't believed him until he had pressed his hand to the invisible barrier that kept him caged within the walls of the fortress.

Like a prisoner.

One who longed to taste the freedom she could eat to her heart's content in this strange valley.

Nina slowly lifted her left arm above her head, so the sleeve of her blouse fell back to reveal her watch. The second hand ticked in a steady rhythm, the sound cutting through the silence. How long had she been in the valley? It felt like hours, but nothing seemed to have changed.

She sat up and frowned at the position of the sun.

It hovered above the mountains.

In exactly the same place it had been when she had entered the valley.

Nina checked the shadows, sure she must be wrong, but their lengths and angles were all the same too.

Did time not move in this valley? She would have thought herself insane to ask that question just hours ago, but now anything seemed possible. But the water flowed and the clouds drifted. It was only the time of day that didn't change.

"Food is being prepared for you."

Nina jumped and quickly looked back over her shoulder, towards the tunnel. Lucifer stood there, shrouded in shadow, the golden light from the torch playing over his handsome features. They were sombre again, clouded in a way she found she didn't like. One that made her want to say or do something to lift the sorrow from his heart.

She rose onto her feet and padded up the short incline to him, stopping on the grass just a few metres from him.

"How long have I been here?" Nina turned and looked back down at the river, watching the water sparkle in the dappled light as it raced around a bend near the bridge.

"In the valley?" he said, his soft voice soothing her almost as much as the sun on her skin and the beauty surrounding her.

More so in fact.

It comforted her, chasing away the lingering trace of fear in her veins. When she looked at the red bridge to the forest now, she wasn't afraid of what might be in those woods.

She felt safe with Lucifer standing at her back.

She felt he would protect her.

A ridiculous notion. She barely knew the man. Just because he had protected her once, didn't mean he would do it again. And what was there out here that she needed protection from anyway? There was nothing in this valley but her.

And Lucifer.

She turned her face towards him but stopped just short of looking at him, keeping her profile angled slightly away from him instead. She felt his gaze on her face, slowly roaming it and then lower, igniting that low burn in her blood that she felt sure would always be there when he looked at her.

She nodded.

"Fourteen hours." He sounded distant. Lost in thought?

Lost in looking at her?

A blush climbed her cheeks and she looked away from him, needing a moment to compose herself so she could focus on what was important. It didn't feel as if she had been here fourteen hours, but she had lost track of time. She checked her watch again and frowned as the second hand ticked past the minute mark.

If she had been here fourteen hours, it should be dark. Presuming time moved in the same way here as it did back in London.

Heck, she really had lost her mind if she was beginning to believe it was possible she was in a place where time flowed at a different pace.

"Does it ever grow dark?" She lifted her gaze to the bright orb in the sky. Was that even real? Was any of it? What if it was all just an incredible illusion and she was really standing in another grim black room?

Or the valley was in fact as dark and bleak as that land she had seen beyond the trees?

Did Lucifer have the power to make that happen?

He had said that he had created this place.

When he didn't answer her question, she looked over her right shoulder at him and found him staring off into the distance.

"It can," he murmured and his eyes slowly dropped to rest on her, losing their glassy quality and gaining a sharp edge that pierced her with its intensity and sent a bolt of heat shooting through her blood. "But why would you desire to see the darkness?"

Nina supposed it was a strange question considering that she hadn't enjoyed her time inside the gothic fortress, shut away and unable to leave. She had made it painfully clear to Lucifer that it felt like a cell to her too, and that she craved light and air. Freedom. Now she wanted it to be dark. Why?

"It just seems strange as it is," she whispered and then found some strength to place into her words as his eyes narrowed on her, a flicker of curiosity in them. "The sun never moves... the stars never shine... the seasons probably remain the same. Time never flows. It's static and you must grow bored of seeing it always the same?"

Lucifer's eyes left her, returning to the valley and remaining there, the distant edge back in them. He looked absorbed in the scenery, but she knew he was thinking about what she had said and she feared she had overstepped the mark and offended him by finding a flaw with this place of his creation.

"Do you desire to see the stars?" He didn't look at her, not even when she nodded.

He looked taller in the shadows, wrapped up in them, with only the flickering light of the torch illuminating his face. He looked as if he belonged in the inky black with them, and she began to feel he had been asking about more than the valley when he had asked why she desired to see the darkness.

"I do want to see the stars, Lucifer," she said and his golden gaze fell to her, narrowing slightly, as if hearing his name leaving her lips had been as thrilling as when she heard hers leaving his. She pressed on, wanting to get her point across before her nerve failed. She was sure she might offend him, but she couldn't let fear of that deter her. She wanted to talk to him and the valley had opened up an avenue of conversation. She also wanted to know why this place remained as it was. "I want to see the stars but that wasn't my point. My point was that nothing changes in this valley. I've been here fourteen hours by your calculation and nothing has changed. It all remains the same. The temperature. The position of the sun. The sound of the river. The breeze. Everything here is static."

"Static," he murmured and stared across at the mountains. His expression darkened, the black slashes of his eyebrows drawing together, turning his golden irises a full shade closer to amber. Those eyes slid down to her, piercing her with their intensity and stealing her breath. "Not everything here is static. You are not. You are changed."

Nina felt keenly in that moment that she had. Seeing the valley and discovering more about Lucifer had changed her. She was no longer afraid of him or the castle, but she didn't understand why. Perhaps understanding was part of the reason. She felt she knew a piece of him now. She felt there was a part of them that was the same.

They were kindred spirits.

"If I show you the stars, will you be inclined to leave this place and dine with me?"

Her eyes leaped to meet his, her heart stuck on the part where he had asked her to dinner while her head screamed at her to focus on the first part of what he had said—the part about the stars. The logical part of her won and she looked up at the blue vault above her.

"I would, but is it really possible?" Her eyes scanned the scattered clouds and their backdrop. A star could never penetrate such light. Not even a planet had the brightness to shine through the strength of the sun here.

But Lucifer had said she could see the stars. He had offered to make them shine for her but she still wasn't sure how that was possible.

He moved behind her and she looked back at him, her chest aching as she caught the sorrow in his amber eyes as he stared beyond her at the valley. He raised his left hand and she wanted to press hers to it, wanted to feel his fingers slide between hers and close over her knuckles, needed him to know that he wasn't alone.

She was here with him.

He pressed his palm to the invisible barrier that stopped him from entering a valley of his own creation and closed his eyes. The muscles of his jaw popped, his sensual lips compressing into a thin line as he frowned, his eyebrows drawing tight together. His nose wrinkled, his top lip drawing off his teeth in a grimace that spoke of pain.

Pain she wanted to ease.

He was hurting himself with whatever he was doing.

Why?

Nina took a step towards him but stopped dead when his canines lengthened. She blinked, sure she was imagining things, but they remained longer, almost like small fangs.

Lucifer grunted and made a sound that was close to a snarl, and she swore the shadows in the tunnel flickered and moved, dancing around him like smoke.

The light dipped.

She whirled to face the valley, her eyes growing enormous as a shiver ran down her spine and thighs.

It was changing.

Her lips parted, the shivers growing in intensity as she stood on the brow of the hill, awed by the sight before her.

The air grew cooler as the sky rapidly changed, the sun drifting lower towards the mountains to her right and the forest there. Another shiver danced down her back as the white cragged peaks of the mountain changed to gold and threads of pink and yellow laced the fluffy clouds as they all raced to her right. The blue vault turned orange beyond the mountains and then a rainbow of colours burst upwards, from pink to yellow to green and then the deepest blue she had ever seen.

Her breath hitched as the sun sank below the cragged peaks on her right and a huge full moon rose on the left side of the valley. It glowed red as it ascended into the darkening sky and slowly turned orange and then paled to a white so bright that it hurt her eyes, but she couldn't make herself tear them away from its beauty, not even to see the valley stretching below her bathed in blue hues.

Stars emerged, one by one, gradually brightening until they broke through the light of the moon to shine above her, like nothing she had ever seen before.

A chill erupted across her skin as she tipped her head back, her breath lodging in her throat and her heart pounding as she took in the most beautiful heavens she had ever witnessed.

She was amazed.

Bewitched.

Her gaze followed the spine of the Milky Way above her, her mind numbed by the beauty of it, empty of thought as she stood beneath it and tried to take it in.

It was incredible.

A laugh bubbled up, born of the joy bursting to life in her heart, and she turned to face Lucifer to thank him for what he had done, because he had done it purely for her.

That laugh died as her eyes met his. They were intent and focused on her, sending a different sort of shiver through her, an awareness of him that stole her breath.

"Is it to your liking?" he whispered and drew his hand away from the barrier, lowering it to his side.

Nina nodded and swallowed hard as she realised something. He was to her liking too. He was handsome, charming and considerate. He had been treating her well and taking care of her, all because he had found her outside his home. She knew that now. He was the one who had found her and had brought her inside to protect her, but she still didn't know why she was here or who had taken her, or if it had anything to do with her ex-husband and his demand that she return to him.

She still only had a vague memory of the events that had happened and it frightened her.

Lucifer shot his left hand out and grasped the wall there.

Nina gasped and rushed into the tunnel, grabbing him by his waist before he could collapse.

He snarled and pushed her away, sending her back out into the valley.

"I am fine," he bit out and glared at her. "It is none of your concern."

It struck her that she was concerned. She was concerned because she had wanted to see the stars and now he looked as pale as those orbs that twinkled above her, drained of colour.

"Return with me." His gruff command echoed along the corridor as he turned and strode away into the darkness.

Nina lingered, able to understand why he was upset but unwilling to obey his orders. She hated it when she showed weakness around anyone too. She didn't like to let people see her vulnerable. Not anymore. Not for a long time.

She drew down a few deep breaths and turned her back to the castle, giving herself a minute to smooth out her feelings and admire the stars that he had made just for her.

No one had ever given her a more beautiful gift and it seemed a shame that she had to leave them. It felt as if she was wasting what he had given her, what had taken him great effort to change for her, but she also didn't want to leave Lucifer alone up there in the castle, waiting for her.

Could she come back tomorrow?

If she did, would the stars still be here or would the valley have changed back to day?

She stared at the moon, charting its position by the peaks of the mountains below it, and realised that, just like the sun, it wasn't moving. It gave her hope that the stars would still be here when she returned.

Nina slipped her tights on, her eyes on the sky the whole time, and then backed towards the tunnel. She knew the moment she crossed the threshold without even looking. A sense of coldness ran through her, a feeling that unsettled her. She pulled the wooden torch from the holder mounted on the black wall, turned away from the valley with a heart that felt heavy in her chest, and trudged along the corridor towards her room in the castle.

The heaviness in her heart began to lift the closer she came to that room, the cold sensation chased away by heat that steadily grew inside her as her thoughts turned away from the valley and back to Lucifer.

A greeting balanced on her lips as she stepped through the door at the other end and died as she realised that she was alone.

Nina padded across the room to a white-cloth-covered dining table that had been set up near the fireplace. Two candlesticks, each holding six black candles, provided the only light, casting a golden glow over the food on the serving trays beneath them.

And the single place setting.

She placed the wooden torch down into the unlit fireplace, turned back to the table, and idly ran her fingers over the empty end, her thoughts with Lucifer.

Where had he gone?

She had upset him, and she didn't know how. She wanted to leave the room and go in search of him, but she rounded the table instead and sat at the opposite end to the one Lucifer should have occupied.

The heaviness returned to her heart as she stared at that spot, easily imagining him there with her, dining with her and perhaps even talking to her about things other than the man who had taken her and who might want to hurt her.

If he talked about himself, maybe she would find the courage to tell him about herself too.

Maybe she would finally lower her guard for the first time in years and let someone inside.

And neither of them would be alone anymore.

CHAPTER 8

Lucifer flashed his fangs at a lower demon as he appeared near the prison. The hideous creature scuttled away into the shadows and hissed at him from behind a rock. He flicked his left hand towards it and black blood splattered the ground where the demon had been. Vile little bastards. He did despise the lesser creatures of his realm.

Especially when they were dragging him away from something pleasant, something he desired to do with every drop of his blood, and were forcing him to deal with something repulsive instead.

He eyed the three male brown-skinned scaly demons kneeling in the circle in the black courtyard of the prison ahead of him, surrounded by six of his finest Hell's angels. The demons' huge yellow eyes all locked on him, their rough throats working on hard swallows as they spotted him. The spines that ran up their arms trembled in a wave like motion, revealing their fear to him. The one in the middle flicked his forked blue tongue out to wet wide lips.

His own men were equally as restless, their red feathered wings shifting constantly, a bright bloody backdrop for their crimson-edged obsidian armour. Two of them held curved black blades pointed at the three demons. Two stood behind them to ensure they didn't attempt to escape.

The remaining two broke away, approaching him as he glared at the demons and did his best to ignore how bleak his realm looked when compared with the valley where he had left Nina.

Nina.

Fuck, he had wanted to dine with her. A stupid and ridiculous desire, one that showed only weakness and deserved to be crushed out of existence. If his men learned he was falling for a mere slip of a mortal, they would mutiny.

Falling?

Lucifer blinked at that and then growled as darkness surged within him to eradicate the insane notion and replace it with something more fitting.

Lusting after.

Never falling.

He had vowed to never fall again, and it was a vow he meant to keep.

Nina was beautiful, a very attractive little human, and if she wasn't part of his enemy's plan, he would gladly fuck her and might even keep her around for a spell.

But she was part of Mihail's plan, whether she knew it or not, and he had to remember that.

He reached the courtyard and snarled again as he felt the familiar tug in his chest, the one that pulled him back towards his fortress behind him.

His golden gaze sought the towering black block of the prison to his right, followed the drop on the open side of the cells that plunged into a boiling river of lava so broad the prisoners couldn't even attempt to leap from the cells to escape them. Not that it stopped some from trying and burning in the river. He scanned from there to the courtyard and then off to his left, following the invisible line that marked the boundary of his own personal cell.

The imprisonment imposed upon him by his failure to defeat Apollyon in their last match was fading, allowing him to stretch the limits of his cell, but it was still powerful. It hindered him and stopped him from going where he pleased in his own damned realm.

It had irked him before, in the millennia when he had been allowing the angel to win and keep him imprisoned in the bottomless pit in order to stop the princes of Hell from escaping into the mortal realm and beyond. It pissed him off now that those same princes had escaped the boundaries of Hell and were free.

It pissed him off now that he had seen the valley again.

His thoughts drifted back to it as he issued orders to his men to retrieve information from the three demons who had been allied with the princes. Information was more important now than ever. It was only a matter of time before Heaven desired knowledge on the princes in order to aid their attempt to locate the four rogue fallen angels.

Lucifer wanted all the information that he could get on the bastards, and then he would make Heaven pay dearly for it and his help.

They would have to bargain for it.

He smiled grimly and watched the two senior Hell's angels go to work on the demons, using their claws to shred the flesh of one and force the other two to talk in order to avoid the same treatment. He had trained his men well. It wasn't long before one of the demons broke, muttering panicked things to himself about the princes.

Lucifer stepped forwards, his own black nails growing into claws as he approached the babbling brown-skinned demon.

A flash of Nina standing in the valley stopped him in his tracks.

She had looked beautiful bathed in sunlight.

Breathtaking.

It had threaded her rich auburn hair with gold and the way she had smiled at him, her face aglow with happiness, had almost brought a smile to his lips too.

Had almost given him a share of that joy that had shone in her pale green eyes.

It had faded before taking hold though, driven away by the sight of the valley. It had been centuries since he had locked the doors and shut that small slice of paradise away, because it was a paradise that felt like Hell to him now.

It was a place he had made but couldn't step into while he was under the laws of Heaven.

He could only enter it in the times when he had won against Apollyon, securing his freedom for a few centuries. He had created it as a substitute for the mortal realm after realising his power negatively affected that fragile world whenever he ventured into it, even when he tried to contain it, and he had no desire to end that plane.

So he had spent time in his valley instead.

Lucifer lowered his hands to his sides and looked at his men, silently issuing them orders to continue with their interrogation.

He didn't feel like bloodying his hands today.

He backed off a few steps, an unfamiliar heaviness pressing down on his chest.

In his mind, he didn't see the three demons as his men terrorised them, spilling their vile black blood onto the bleak obsidian ground.

He saw Nina standing in the valley, surrounded by nature, seemingly at one with the beauty.

As if she had been made for that place.

For him.

She was light with a seed of darkness inside her heart.

He was darkness with a flicker of light.

A sigh escaped him and the yellow eyes of the demon on the right of the three narrowed in a way he didn't like, one that said the male knew something was affecting him and he wasn't his usual self.

Lucifer flicked his left hand forwards and the male's head exploded, showering black blood and bone over three of his men and the demon beside him. One of Lucifer's men looked back at him and he snarled, flashing his fangs as his eyes briefly burned crimson, warning the wretch to return to his work before he suffered the same fate as the demon.

The fallen angel wisely obeyed.

Lucifer huffed and tried to keep his mind off Nina and the valley, but it was impossible. She constantly filled his head, was all he could think about and had been from the moment he had set eyes on her in the courtyard.

He tried to focus on something else, but the something else his mind chose was the valley, and he immediately pictured her in it.

It had given him both joy and pain to take Nina there. Joy he had gained from seeing how much she enjoyed the world of his creation. Pain he had gained from being unable to remain there with her as she had wished.

He looked over his shoulder, his gaze scanning the winding path that cut across the cragged bleak land to the spires of rock that rose in a curved wall around the courtyard of his fortress. A fortress that had towers so high their roofs melted into the dark ceiling of Hell.

His home.

She waited there.

For him?

Fuck, if he was feeling honest with himself, he had been waiting for her the entire fourteen hours she had been in the valley. He had tried to work, had attempted to focus on his duties and the things that required his attention. In the end, he had drifted around the castle, feeling for the first time just how cold and empty it could be.

Because he had wanted to be elsewhere.

With her.

He turned back to face the castle, filled with a pressing need to return to her. It had nothing to do with seeing her again, or hearing her voice, or smelling the soft fragrance of her fading perfume.

It had everything to do with business. He needed to return to her and ensure that she was obeying his command to stay in her apartment, and also to see if she had remembered anything else about Mihail.

His men were under strict orders not to enter her room and to teleport if she dared to venture into the corridors or other rooms, but the chances of her seeing one of them in their natural form of an angel was still too high for his liking. She seemed to take seeing his powers in her stride, was coping well with the things he had revealed to her to test her mind and see whether perhaps he could push her a little again to make her remember things, but he knew that if she saw his men for what they really were, it would be too much. It would break her.

That was the only reason he was returning and the only reason he was keeping her locked away.

It had nothing to do with any sort of desire to protect her or spend time with her.

He walked the snaking path back to the fortress, his gaze on it the entire time, shutting out the black lands around him.

It would have been quicker to teleport, but shifting the passage to the separate plane where the valley existed from its original location to Nina's room, and then turning day into night for her had expended a vast amount of his powers, weakening him. Looking back, he should have walked to the prison and teleported back, but he had wanted to reach it quickly.

Because he had wanted to return to her.

Lucifer shoved that thought out of his head and clenched his fists to stop them from trembling. He cursed the sign of weakness, one he hoped his men hadn't noticed. It was only temporary. Within the hour, he would be back at full strength.

If he had realised that altering the valley would drain him so fiercely, he wouldn't have done it.

He snorted at that.

Fuck, he could even taste his own lies now.

He would have done it even if it had killed him.

He would have done it because he had wanted nothing else in that moment than seeing the pleasure and astonishment he had known Nina would feel on seeing the stars and the valley bathed in moonlight.

He had wanted to impress her.

"You seem awfully distracted today." The deep male voice coming from his left instantly drove thoughts of Nina from his mind and he teleported a short distance on instinct, placing some land between him and the angel.

Mihail.

"Venturing beyond the boundaries of your prison again?" Mihail ran ice-blue eyes over him and shifted his weight to maintain his balance on the tall basalt rock near the path.

Lucifer sneered at him for daring to look down on him and flexed his fingers at his sides, his claws emerging as he thought about bringing the angel down to the level where he belonged.

Under Lucifer's feet.

"I am well within the boundary." He calmly pointed to the invisible wall that surrounded him but Mihail's cold eyes didn't move from him.

The angel spread his glossy pure white wings, an intimidation tactic that might work on the lower angels, but failed to make an impact on Lucifer. The span of Mihail's wings was nothing compared with that of his own.

The wings he had once possessed anyway.

Now he possessed only a shadow of them, but they were both beautiful and terrifying, fitting for a king of Hell.

They burst from his back, ripping through the fine material of his suit jacket, and he spread them. The black shadows fluttered, forming shapes like feathers for the briefest of moments before shifting and regrouping, in a constant state of flux. Their span exceeded that of Mihail's wings and the angel raised a pale eyebrow at him, his eyes turning colder as he glared at Lucifer. It seemed the little servant of Heaven hadn't realised he possessed wings again.

He now possessed far more than mere wings.

Lucifer threw his right hand forwards, unleashing a black orb of energy that shot directly towards Mihail. The angel's icy eyes widened and he kicked off, launching into the air just as the orb struck the rock. It exploded, blasting black fragments in all directions. Mihail grunted as the tiny splinters hit the backs of his bare thighs, each leaving a red streak on his golden skin.

None touched Lucifer.

They bounced off the invisible wall of his power and onto the black ground, tumbling away from him.

"An unprovoked attack?" Mihail sneered at him, beating his broad white wings to keep him stationary in the air. His black armour seemed to suck all light from around him, making the dull white inlay stand out, revealing the pictures of demons being defeated by men carved on it. "That is rather like you."

"I did not think you had come to talk." Lucifer threw his other hand forwards, unleashing another ball of energy that expanded as it rocketed towards the angel.

Mihail beat his wings and shot left, evading it, his long white ponytail streaming over his right shoulder.

"I have not." The angel halted in the air again and drew a white blade from it. "I have come to take the mortal female from you."

Lucifer frowned at that.

Why would the bastard want to take her back rather than use her against him?

It didn't matter.

It wasn't going to happen.

Lucifer lowered his head and glared through his lashes at the angel hovering above him, his lips peeling back off his emerging fangs as he growled.

Nina was under his protection now.

He wouldn't surrender her to Mihail.

Mihail quirked a pale eyebrow at him, curiosity crossing his wretched face for a heartbeat before it turned to horror.

Lucifer pressed his wrists together and shoved both of his hands forwards, snarling as he unleashed a blast of black energy directly at the angel. Mihail attempted to dodge it, but it caught his right wing and sent him tumbling through the air. Lucifer didn't give him a chance to recover. He kicked off and beat his shadow wings, shooting towards the angel as he attempted to right himself.

He roared as he pulled a flaming black blade out of the air at his side and launched it in a sweeping curve, aiming straight for Mihail's neck. Mihail's blue eyes grew enormous and he twisted at the waist, his bare stomach rippling with the effort to turn himself in time. His white blade came up and Lucifer snarled out his fury as it blocked his strike and pressed forwards, driving the angel backwards through the air.

Mihail grunted and tried to shove forwards to counter him.

No use.

Lucifer grinned and swept his arm out and the angel went flying backwards, sailing through the air with his wings streaming past him and the most wonderfully shocked look on his face.

A jolt of pleasure ran through Lucifer, igniting a hunger to see the angel begging for mercy at his feet.

He beat his wings, each sweep of them gaining urgency, born of that hunger to finally defeat the one angel capable of defeating him.

Mihail hit the enormous black spires of stone that surrounded the courtyard, but not as Lucifer had anticipated it. The male struck them with his feet first, coming into a vertical crouch, and kicked off. The force of the pressure he exerted to launch himself back towards Lucifer cracked the rock and Lucifer growled as a whole spire collapsed, crashing into the courtyard.

He had only just fixed it up after Asmodeus had killed a fucking dragon in it, the creature's lava-like blood destroying half of the pavement.

Lucifer flew harder, clutching his sword in his left hand and hurling his right one forward to unleash another blast of energy. He put more of his power into it this time, all of his fury and hunger to kill.

It shot towards Mihail, expanding rapidly until it was three times the size of the angel, easily able to swallow him whole.

Mihail rolled at the last second, spiralling out of the path of the orb.

Leaving it on a direct course for Lucifer's castle.

Nina.

"No!" Lucifer bellowed and teleported in an instant, reappearing in the path of the blast, between it and the fortress.

He sent his sword away and shoved both hands forwards, at the orb shooting towards him, and braced himself for contact, focusing all of his power on his hands so he could contain the orb and attempt to change its course.

It hit him hard and he grunted as the blow knocked the air from his lungs and hurled him backwards. The energy seared his palms, hotter than the boiling lakes of Hell, and he gritted his teeth as his suit jacket caught fire, rapidly burning away and taking his shirt with it, leaving only tatters behind. Shadows streamed from his arms, sinking deep into the orb.

The fortress loomed behind him and Lucifer growled as he beat his wings, twin feelings he hadn't experienced in a long time surfacing within him to devour him as he struggled with the ball of dark energy.

Despair.

Desperation.

He had to stop it from striking the castle.

He couldn't fail.

If he did, Nina could be injured.

Or worse.

He threw his head back and roared as he flew harder, each desperate beat of his wings draining his strength, making him shake from weakness, until he was struggling to breathe. Fear closed his throat. Despair and doubt filled his heart, mocking him. He was going to fail again.

He was going to fail her.

He was going to kill her.

Never.

He would protect Nina with his life if it came to it.

His hands began to melt into the black ball of energy and he cried out as it burned him again, destroying his fingers first before it ate away at his palms, gnawing up to his wrists. He shoved more desperately, his teeth gritted against the pain and his fangs cutting into his lower lip. It was no use. He couldn't slow the blast enough, not even with his shadows countering it, attempting to consume the energy back into him.

He looked back at the castle.

There was only one thing he could do, but it would leave him vulnerable to Mihail. The angel would easily be able to kill him, and then he would take Nina.

Lucifer realised he was going to lose no matter what he did.

And he didn't like it.

It brought memories back to the surface, pain that refused to die and haunted him every day of his life.

He had been filled with such cold certainty before in his long existence.

Back when he had realised that no matter what he did, he would not escape the pit and he would not be allowed to return to his beloved home in Heaven.

But this time he had a choice.

He could choose to save Nina.

He could sacrifice himself for her sake.

She was worthy of such an act.

He focused all of his power, digging his shadows into the orb to anchor it to him, and teleported.

He reappeared close the plateau, with his back to the wall of rock that supported it, facing the castle. It shimmered through the black orb, just visible to him. The last of his strength left him and his shadows faded, but he kept his eyes on the fortress and his thoughts with Nina as his grip on the orb disappeared.

The energy pulsed over him and he tossed his head back, arching violently forwards as he bellowed in agony, so loud the ground trembled and the air vibrated with his roar.

Pain devoured him.

It ate his awareness of anything but it, blazed so deep in his bones that he was sure they were burning to ashes just as his hands had, that he was going to be consumed by his own power and this was the end for him.

Numbness followed it.

And then voices.

He cracked his sore eyes open, trying to seek the source of those voices, sure that it was Mihail and his men come to kill him.

A broadly-built male with familiar black hair and golden eyes towered over him, his obsidian armour as glossy as the raven wings furled against his back.

Beside him, a petite hazel-eyed female lingered, her hand clasping his and the softness in her gaze making Lucifer want to end his own life.

The male nudged him with the toe of his black leather boot.

Asmodeus.

Lucifer bared his fangs at the angel of his own creation and shoved onto his knees, and paused when he saw he had hands again. He stared at them, and then slowly shifted his focus to the woman. Liora. A powerful witch.

She tucked her long chestnut hair behind her ear and smiled, and it was enough to make Lucifer want to vomit.

The witch had restored his hands for him.

The perfect end to a shitty fucking day.

He owed her and she knew it.

It was bad enough that Asmodeus had witnessed everything, and Lucifer knew from the smug look on the maggot's face that he had witnessed *everything*. The fight against Mihail and what had followed as he had attempted to protect his castle from his own energy blast. Not only that, but Mihail was gone.

Meaning Asmodeus had fought him and driven him away.

And now Lucifer owed Asmodeus too.

The black-haired male held his hand out to him and Lucifer growled at it. He had already humiliated himself enough. He wasn't going to add to it.

He carefully rose onto his feet and locked his knees when they tried to betray him and buckle beneath his weight. His shadow wings streamed from his bare back, shifting to counter each sway of his body and keep him steady as his strength slowly returned.

Lucifer flexed his fingers. They were pale and perfect, tipped with short black nails. His bare arms and chest were covered in scratches and lacerations, smeared with black dust and rivulets of red. A snarl tore from his lips.

Mihail would pay.

His snarl died and his head snapped up, his eyes fixing on his fortress.

What if Asmodeus hadn't driven Mihail away?

What if Mihail had left, after taking Nina?

Lucifer stumbled forwards, managing a few steps before his right knee collapsed, sending him back down onto the black ground. He struck it hard and grimaced as pain shot up his knee and zinged through his bones. He couldn't wait for his strength to return. He had to reach Nina.

He had to see that she was still there.

Waiting for him.

He shoved back onto his feet and fixed his eyes on the fortress, determined to reach it. The distance seemed enormous, an insurmountable obstacle between him and his little mortal when he was weak. He wanted to teleport there, straight into the room she had made her own, but no matter how hard he tried to muster it, he didn't have the power to use that ability. His knee went to give out on him again but he managed to remain upright this time, merely staggering a few steps to the right instead.

"You are in no fit condition to walk."

He ignored Asmodeus's observation and kept trudging forwards, unable to deny the fierce need to see that Nina was safe and Mihail hadn't stolen her from him.

When Asmodeus placed his hand on Lucifer's shoulder, Lucifer turned on him with a growl and lashed out at him, backhanding him hard across the face and knocking him away.

Asmodeus snarled right back at him, his golden eyes flashing red and his fangs on show.

There had been a time when Asmodeus had known his place and wouldn't have dared to touch him.

Lucifer huffed.

There had also been a time when Asmodeus had been more like a servant to him, a slave who did his bidding without questioning his orders. He slid his gaze to his right, towards the male, and hated the voice that mocked him by mentioning that he had attempted to do with Asmodeus what his master had done with him. He had made the male carry out atrocities without a thought to how it made him feel and had expected him to obey his every command.

He spat a curse at Asmodeus, one so dark that the ground shook beneath his feet, and instantly regretted it when the trembling caused him to lose his balance and he hit the basalt knees-first again. The small pebbles cut through the remains of his trousers, biting into his knees.

He should have paved every fucking path in his kingdom.

He slammed his fist into the ground, so hard that fault lines forked out from where he had struck and pain danced up his arm, a fiery heat that stole feeling from him for a brief second before he burned in agony all over again.

"Do you mind? Do you know how much of my power it took to remake those?" Liora's light voice was laced with a sharp edge, and as much as Lucifer wanted to lash out at her too, he found he couldn't.

He looked down at the hands she had repaired and realised that it must have taken most of her power to use such a spell. Suddenly, he didn't have the heart to hit anything for a while.

What the fuck was happening to him?

He wanted to blame Erin, but he had the terrible feeling that this time the blame rested on someone else's shoulders.

Someone's beautiful, slender shoulders.

Shoulders that were part of a curvy body hidden beneath prim and proper clothing, and supported a head full of wavy red hair, a face made up of clear skin with rosy cheeks, soft shell-pink lips that he couldn't stop fucking thinking about kissing, and the most stunning peridot eyes that entranced him.

Nina.

Hell, he needed to see her.

He needed it so badly that he took the hand Asmodeus offered, hauling himself back onto his feet, and didn't even grumble when the dark angel cast his other hand out, creating a swirling black maelstrom slightly taller than he was and broader.

Lucifer trudged into the portal, not quite able to believe he was relying on Asmodeus and allowing someone to help him.

That hadn't happened in millennia.

Since long before he had fallen.

No one had ever tried to help him.

He stepped out of the portal in front of his fortress and looked back at Asmodeus and the little witch. She wisely busied herself with the hem of her black dress, fraying it with trembling fingers. The dark angel didn't avoid his gaze. He held it instead, his golden eyes intense and focused.

"Mihail left when we arrived," Asmodeus said, his deep voice suiting his appearance, and grimaced as his eyes darkened to red again. "I wanted to kill the bastard for what he did to Nevar and Lysia, but he fled the moment he saw us approaching."

Lucifer had to bite his tongue to stop himself from asking whether the angel had been alone.

"You have…" He sucked down a deep breath and somehow managed to force the words out. "My gratitude."

Asmodeus looked as if he had just sucker-punched him.

Liora's eyes widened but she kept them locked on her dress. A dress that stretched tight over the swell of her stomach. Lucifer looked at the bump. It seemed his grandson would have a playmate soon.

Everything was going to Hell and he had the awful feeling he was going there with it.

Was nothing sacred?

For thousands of years he had lived for one purpose, to rule his realm and one day have his revenge.

Now he found himself living for visits with his grandson, seeing his daughter, and even the rare visits that Asmodeus made that he knew weren't habit or about the business of tracking the princes of Hell. Asmodeus was losing his fear of him, just as the others were. They were coming to view him as an ally.

A friend.

Hell help him, but he was beginning to view them as something other than enemies too.

Something other than lowly beings put on this planet to amuse him, and sometimes infuriate him.

He waved Asmodeus away and turned towards his fortress. He had made it up the first of the curved polished black stone steps when Asmodeus spoke.

"So who is Nina?"

Lucifer froze.

He could feel the amusement running through his creation's blood, knew the bastard had been ready to gauge his reaction and he had given himself away by stopping dead and tensing on hearing her name.

"A female Mihail brought to me. I am using her as bait for the angel." He schooled his features and looked back at Asmodeus.

The amusement he could sense in him shone in his golden eyes. "Right. She is nothing more than bait. Understood."

Asmodeus turned away, casting another portal at the same time. He ushered Liora towards it and through it, and paused at the threshold.

The black-haired male looked back at him. "You sounded a little concerned about your bait being taken from you when Liora was patching you up... in fact... you seemed a little like you were worried she would be gone... and you look worried that she might be."

Lucifer scowled at the insubordinate bastard. If he'd had a fragment of his power left, he would have had the angel on his knees and pleading him for mercy. As it was, he could barely knock him on his backside and Asmodeus knew it. He was pressing his advantage.

Just as Lucifer had taught him.

Asmodeus waved him away and backed towards the portal, a smile curving his lips. "She is safe. I had Liora check with a spell."

He tried to hide his relief but the chuckle that left Asmodeus's lips said he failed. Lucifer raised his hand, willing to weaken himself a little to knock the angel on his backside after all, but the portal swallowed Asmodeus and disappeared.

"Maggot," Lucifer grumbled and steadily climbed the steps to his home, trying to ignore the fact that the weight on his chest seemed a little less now that he knew Nina was safe.

A diagonal slash above his hip split open as he lifted his left leg to climb the next step and he grunted and covered it with his hand. Warm wetness coated his palm and he pressed harder, stemming the flow of blood. The toe of his left shoe caught on the top of the step and he almost fell, his wings shifting and fluttering to restore his balance.

Lucifer grunted and managed to make it up the remaining steps without falling or reopening any more wounds.

He slowly walked towards the imposing tall twin doors of the fortress and they opened for him, parting to reveal the vestibule and the floating staircases that criss-crossed the vast room.

The candles in the gilded-bone chandeliers flickered as he entered and he walked a little taller as one of his men came out of the corridor across the room from him. The young Hell's angel studied him warily, his crimson eyes darting over his wounds before shooting off to the wall behind him. The male wisely chose to head back into the room he had exited, leaving Lucifer alone in the great hall.

Had the male attempted to help him, Lucifer might have been tempted to send him back to Heaven for his insolence. He wasn't in the mood for company and coddling.

He managed to make it to the first floor of the castle, carefully ascending the steps so he didn't fall off the open sides. In his current condition, he wasn't sure his wings would hold his weight. The last thing he needed was to fall flat on his face and have one of his men witness it. It was rare enough that he came back from a fight with injuries.

Normally, he could heal any injury instantly.

Because normally, he hadn't been expending a vast amount of his power to make day into night in order to impress a human female.

Tonight, he would have to patch them up and allow them to heal at their natural pace.

He couldn't remember the last time he had been forced to do such a thing but he definitely remembered how uncomfortable it had been in the times he'd had to wait for his heightened healing abilities to repair his body.

He was going to be in a sour mood for days.

A sliver of his strength slowly returned, enough that he could walk without fear of collapsing and making a fool of himself. His wings shrank into his bare back and he rolled his shoulders, grimacing as his bones cracked and his body ached. He had never thought he would miss his power to heal instantly, but he would have traded half his kingdom to have it back right now, and not only because the pain was already driving him crazy.

He feared that Mihail would return while he was weakened and snatch Nina from him.

He ascended the stairs to the second floor and followed the balcony that ran around the vestibule to the other side where his quarters were located. Nina's weren't far from his and he had to pass her apartment in order to reach his own one.

He slid a glance at her door as he passed.

It opened and she stood there before him, her peridot eyes growing enormous as they ran down him and took in every inch of his chest.

"What happened?" She stepped forwards before he could tell her to remain in her room, her hands coming up to flutter in front of her as if she wanted to touch him but feared what might happen.

He feared it too.

He wasn't sure he would be able to control himself if she placed her hands on him.

"The man who took you returned. I made sure that he left." He went to turn away but she caught his left arm.

A bolt of electricity shot through his veins from the point where she touched him, burning up his blood and leaving him breathless as he fought to master his urge to turn back to face her, slide his free hand along her jaw and dip his head to kiss her.

He managed to tamp down that need but couldn't stop himself from looking back at her.

She stared at her hand on his arm, her eyes wider than before and her lips parted. He thought she would take her hand away when he moved his arm. She released him, but their skin was only apart for a second before she was touching him again, her fingers lightly dancing over the lacerations on his arm, following each one upwards towards his shoulder.

Making him burn for her.

He bit back a growl born of pleasure not anger and tried to evade her by moving his shoulder back.

It didn't stop her.

It only made things worse.

She stepped fully into the hallway and pursued him, her fingers tracking across his bare chest now, making his heart thump painfully hard against his ribs.

"Did the man do this to you? What did he want?" she said, her stunning gaze filling with a flicker of fear but also concern as she stroked the line of a deeper wound that darted across his left pectoral and over the first set of abdominal muscles.

Her fingers paused.

Her eyes lifted to meet his.

A touch of colour stained her cheeks.

"He wanted you," Lucifer murmured.

Her eyes went a little wider, the colour on her cheeks a little darker, as if she thought he was talking about himself and that he desired her.

His gaze dropped to her sweet lips, parted and open to him, begging for a kiss.

Hell, but he did want her.

And Hell, he would have her.

CHAPTER 9

Nina gasped as Lucifer's lips descended on hers and his hands clamped down on her hips, drawing her towards him. Her arms looped around his neck on instinct, tugging him closer to her as she lost herself for a moment in the heat of his kiss.

The taste of ash and blood on her tongue was a stark reminder of his injuries that threw a bucket of ice on the fire of her desire.

She reluctantly pressed her hands to his shoulders and eased him back. He broke away from her mouth with a soft huff that spoke volumes to her, telling her that he was as happy about stopping the kiss as she was.

Nina looked up at his face, dirty and bloodstained, no longer smooth pale perfection, because of her.

Because he had wanted to protect her.

Golden eyes searched hers, the heat of passion still burning in them, calling her to surrender to the fire that raged inside her too.

She wanted to give in to it.

Heaven help her, but she wanted this man who stood before her, and not only because he was beautiful on the outside.

He was beautiful on the inside too.

She could see beyond the barriers now. A single look into his eyes revealed everything to her. His guard was down, stripped of him as his eyes darted between hers, seeking something unknown, something that she felt sure he was looking for to relieve himself of the feelings she knew he was experiencing.

Because he was just like her.

He didn't want people to see him as he was now. Hurt. Suffering. Bare.

He protected himself with a shield of perfect image and power, but that armour was gone and a different man was looking back at her, one who touched her deep in her heart because he wasn't turning her away. He was letting her see him like this.

He was letting her see him vulnerable and weakened.

She slid her hand down to his and clasped it, and when she stepped back towards her room, he eyed their joined hands with mild surprise in his gaze and then raised it back to hers. He followed her into her apartment, his eyes still darting between hers and a touch of nerves filling them as she led him towards the bathroom beyond the four-poster double bed at the far end of the room.

Part of her expected him to pull away, to bring his shields back up to protect himself.

It humbled her when he didn't.

He allowed her to manoeuvre him into the black-tiled sumptuous bathroom, bringing him to the wide obsidian marble sink that occupied a large section of the vanity unit in front of the huge gilt-framed mirror.

Nina released his hand, reached for the sponge on the dish and ran it under the warm tap. The water grew hot quickly so she switched to filling the bowl with it and adding cold to keep it from scalding her hand as she worked.

Lucifer watched her every move like a hawk, his gaze following her hand as she dipped it into the water, lifted it and squeezed out the sponge.

She brought it towards him and he tensed.

Nina paused, giving him a moment because she could sense that he needed one.

Because she could see that he hadn't accepted help from anyone in a long time and she could relate to that.

When the taut muscles of his chest and stomach relaxed, she gently took hold of his left hand and carefully ran the sponge over it. She kept her eyes fixed on her work as she cleaned away the blood and dirt, revealing smooth pale skin and tiny streaks of red. They were small on his arms, barely scratches, but there were others on his torso that looked as if someone had taken a knife to him.

What had taken place during the fight?

Had Lucifer used his mysterious powers to battle the man?

If he had, did that mean that the man also possessed powers of some sort?

The man had been able to fight Lucifer, had wounded him, badly in some places. That had to mean that he also had powers. It was too much for her to comprehend. She was only just becoming accustomed to the idea that Lucifer might be able to create things with whatever power he possessed. She didn't think she could handle the idea that he also had the ability to use his powers to fight another person.

Another person who was like him.

Lucifer had mentioned that he had driven the man away again, and that caused a heavy feeling in the pit of her stomach because it told her something that terrified her.

Whoever the man was, he was as powerful as Lucifer.

He had been able to stand his ground against him.

And he was after her.

Nina pushed those thoughts away, bringing her focus back to Lucifer and using her work to keep her mind off the man and her predicament. Lucifer had protected her again and she was safe here in his castle. She was sure of that. Once she had him patched up, she would ask about the man and make him explain what was happening.

Lucifer didn't seem to notice the pain as she cleaned his arm and began to head towards his chest. If he did feel anything, he didn't show it. His gaze drifted to her when she had finished his shoulder and started on his pectorals, burning her with its intensity. She kept her eyes on her work, but it didn't stop the blush from scalding her cheeks when she thought about how he had kissed her.

How it had made her feel.

Fired up.

Hungry for more.

She wanted him, and even though she wasn't sure it was wise to sleep with him, she felt powerless to resist his pull and the lure of surrendering to her attraction to him. For the first time in years, she wanted to ignore the sensible part of herself and embrace the impulsive one.

She wanted to risk being hurt again.

Because something told her that Lucifer might be worth that risk.

She glanced up to find his gaze on her lips, dark with hunger that echoed within her. It took all of her willpower to force herself to continue and focus on cleaning him and then the task of binding his wounds. He was in no fit state for the things he was thinking about.

Things she couldn't stop thinking about too, imagining them locked in each other's arms, tangled in a passionate embrace.

It became harder to resist acting out those thoughts when she reached his stomach. She needed a moment to rein in her desires. Her gaze strayed to the hard compact muscles of his abdomen and heat pooled in her belly, drifted lower to the apex of her thighs. Lucifer muttered something, his voice dark magic as he leaned towards her.

She turned her cheek, her eyes fixing on the dirty water in the sink, but it didn't stop him. It only made it worse for her. Her eyes rolled closed as he kissed her jaw and then her neck, his lips trailing fire down it, sending shiver after shiver cascading down her spine. A moan slipped from her lips and she bit her tongue, trying to contain the groan of pleasure.

Lucifer's hands caught her waist.

Nina drew in a deep breath and somehow managed to press her hands to his chest and push him back.

His wounded look cut her to her heart and she glanced down at the chiselled muscles of his chest before finding the strength to lift her eyes back to his.

"I need to get these wounds clean. What if they get infected?" She busied herself with draining the dirty water from the sink, rinsing the bowl, and filling it again.

Lucifer stared at her the entire time, his silence making the air around her too thick to breathe. She wanted him too, he had to know that, but she couldn't rush into this. She needed to give him time to heal. It wasn't as if she was going anywhere.

Her eyebrows shot up.

When had she stopped thinking about leaving?

It was all she had wanted for the entire time she had been locked in the fortress, was all she had thought about, born of a desire to protect Lucifer from whatever her ex-husband might have planned for him.

But now the thought of leaving hurt her.

Her eyes slowly lifted to Lucifer's face.

The thought of leaving him pained her.

His eyes narrowed and dropped to her lips, and she couldn't resist him as he pulled her into his arms and claimed her mouth again. She surrendered to him this time, allowing him to tug her against his chest as his lips dominated her, filling her with heat and hunger that burned so fiercely she feared they would consume her.

When he tugged her even closer, banding his arms around her and crushing her to his chest, forcing her to tip her head back to keep their mouths together, he grunted.

The sharp sound of pain leaving his lips drove awareness back into her mind, pushing it through the haze of desire like a spear of light.

Nina sighed and didn't have to push him back this time. He set her away from him and glared down at his chest, as if his injuries were more of an inconvenience than anything else.

"We should finish patching you up," she whispered, and was that her voice sounding so breathless and needy?

Her fingers trailed over his chest, following the line of the nastiest cut that dashed over his pectoral and the first pair of abdominal muscles. Heck, he was perfect. She had never seen a body like his, had never looked at a man and felt this level of need purely from gazing at him.

She wanted to give in to that need, but that logical part of her mind was screaming at her again, demanding she place his welfare above her desire to get him naked.

Dark golden eyes lifted to meet hers, the wide abysses of his pupils speaking to her of his need. A need that clearly matched her own.

She had to force herself to look away and focus on her task again. The sponge floated in the clean water, calling her back to her duty. She had started taking care of him and she was determined to finish it, no matter how easily he could sway her into neglecting it again. No matter how many times she had to stop him, she would keep finding the strength to do it.

Nina picked up the sponge, squeezed it out and stared at it, awareness of what came next dawning on her.

She had to keep cleaning his stomach.

She wasn't sure she could do it without her need to kiss him overpowering her again.

Not on the mouth this time.

She wanted to trail her lips down the taut ridges of his stomach, swirl her tongue around the sensual dip of his navel, and follow that treasure trail of dark hair that led down into the waistband of his black trousers.

Nina coughed to clear her throat, shoved that thought out of her head before it did wreck her fragile control, and set to work on cleaning his other arm. She would build back up to his stomach. Arm first. Then his back. And finally the delicious and tempting ropes of his stomach.

She carefully cleaned his arm, trying to ignore the heat of his gaze as he watched her work. When she had finished moving down from his shoulder to his hand, she paused with her fingers supporting his and stared at his black nails. They looked natural. She rubbed her thumb over them, taking in their perfection.

Lucifer drew his hand away from her and lowered it to his side, and she sensed that if she tried to look at his nails again, he would resort to hiding his hands behind his back as he had before.

Why?

She had been astonished by them when she had first noticed them, but now she was merely curious. She was curious about a lot of things regarding the man stood before her, silently watching her, his chest rising and falling at a steady pace.

That curiosity only grew as she stepped around him and caught sight of his back.

Her eyes darted over the multitude of long silvery streaks on his back and the two thick ridges of scar tissue that ran vertically down his shoulder blades in line with his spine, each around twelve inches long

"Good God, what happened to you?" she whispered.

Lucifer snarled at her.

Really snarled.

Like an animal.

She lifted her head and caught a flash of him in the mirror before he shifted his face away from her.

Her mouth turned dry.

She hadn't slept in hours. That was the only reason she had seen red eyes in that mirror. She was imagining things now. He couldn't possibly have red eyes.

He whirled to face her, his eyes closed and head tilted downwards, and barked out, "I can wash my own damned back."

Nina flinched away from him and then rallied, setting her jaw and glaring at him. Someone had done something terrible to him, had put him through living Hell by the looks of his back, but that was no reason for him to snap at her. She sighed as the part of her that cared for him, that felt they were kindred spirits, whispered that she would have lashed out too if the scars she carried on her heart were visible on her skin and he had seen them. She knew he felt more vulnerable than ever, and she needed him to know that she wasn't going to take advantage of that. She wouldn't judge him or probe into what had happened to him.

She wouldn't push him.

She would take care of him, would tend to him until he realised that she didn't think those marks on his back made him weak.

They made him a survivor, like her.

They made him strong.

"I'll wash it for you, Lucifer. I won't ask any more questions about it or you. It just took me by surprise." Because the rest of him was perfect. Not a scar marring his pale skin.

Someone had gone to war on his back though.

She glanced in the mirror, drawn to looking at it, filled with a pressing need to see the worst of the two scars again—the ones that formed matching lines over his shoulders.

When he didn't move, she whispered, "Lucifer?"

The muscles in his jaw popped, his lips compressing into a thin line, and his nose wrinkled with his frown. Her eyes flitted over his face and then down to his hands as he clenched his fists and his arms trembled at his sides. Whatever he was thinking, she wanted him to stop, because it was clearly hurting him.

Was he remembering what had happened to him?

Her heart kicked in her chest at the thought he might be.

"Lucifer," she softly murmured, set the sponge down on the black vanity unit and cupped both of his cheeks. She tilted his head up. "Look at me, Lucifer."

His eyes slowly opened and hers widened.

A corona of red edged his golden irises.

"I won't ask. I promise. I just want to take care of you."

He swallowed hard and looked away from her, off to his right and the open door there. A bolt of fear shot through her, panic that he might leave. She held his cheeks more firmly, hoping to bring him back to her, because she didn't want him to walk out of that door.

She didn't want to be left alone, wondering what he was doing, knowing that he would be feeling lonely too.

"Please, Lucifer. Let me take care of you."

His eyes shifted back to meet hers and the red was gone, but she knew she hadn't imagined it. There was something about this man, something incredible. Unique. Powerful. During the time he had been away from her, she had thought about everything he had done for her and revealed to her. She had thought him some sort of mage.

Now she felt certain he was more than that.

She just didn't know what.

But she wanted to know.

If she asked, would he tell her?

The soft imploring edge to his steady gaze asked her to hold true to what she had said and not question him. She would do that for him, but she couldn't promise that she would be able to hold her tongue forever.

She needed to know more about him.

Because she was falling in love with him.

CHAPTER 10

Lucifer stared down into Nina's eyes, a rush of emotions threatening to sweep him away and wash away some of the darkness in his heart at the same time. They poured through him, too strong for him to handle even as he braced himself and tried to master them. No matter what he did, they refused to fade while he was looking into Nina's soft gaze, seeing a wealth of warmth and tenderness in her eyes that he didn't deserve.

If she knew how he came to have the scars on his back, would she look at him with so much compassion in her eyes?

No.

He wasn't a fool, and he wouldn't allow his emerging emotions to make him one. He knew that he had done unforgivable things.

Did unforgivable things.

No mortal could comprehend what he was, who he was, and the things that he did as part of his duty. Nina would never understand the path he had trod, sometimes because of blind faith and sometimes by his own choosing. She would never understand him, no matter how much he desired that.

Her peridot eyes shifted slightly, veering right towards his shoulder, and he could easily read her desire to see his back again.

He had kept it hidden for centuries.

None of his men had ever seen it.

None of his lovers.

He had never been naked before anyone.

He had been careful to make sure it never happened, always remaining in his opened shirt and trousers whenever he took a lover.

He had thought he had done it to keep them from seeing the evidence of his sins, the marks that fuelled him and kept him walking the dark path towards vengeance. He had thought he had done it to keep things simple, to stop whoever he was fucking from opening their mouths to ask about the scars.

He had thought wrong.

He turned his cheek to Nina but she refused to surrender, keeping her palms against his face, her warm touch giving him a sliver of comfort that countered the crushing weight of pain as he realised the real reason he had been careful to hide the scars from everyone.

He was ashamed of them.

They were a living reminder of the sins he had committed, the suffering he had caused and had endured. They were a reminder of the atrocities that had befallen him at the hands of demons.

They weren't a sign of strength.

They were a reminder of weakness.

And they made him feel that weakness right down to his soul.

They made him feel vulnerable.

And he hated it.

He curled his fingers back into fists at his sides, unable to bring himself to look at Nina or answer her plea. He wasn't sure how to process what she had said or what she was asking of him.

He wasn't sure he could ever allow someone to take care of him.

He was vile.

As wretched as they came.

He had faltered on the path he had vowed to walk, a path that may have led to his redemption if only he had been strong enough to keep inching forwards up the impossible incline rather than taking one of the many paths that seemed to have run downhill.

One of the many easy routes.

He hadn't been strong enough.

He was weak.

He had been tested, put through trial after trial, and he had failed.

Lucifer closed his eyes and swallowed hard, the pain in his heart making it impossible to breathe as he thought about how differently things might have been. The possibility that he might have been able to redeem himself and return to Heaven still haunted him. It never relented. It was forever there in the back of his mind, deep in his heart, burning in his blackened soul.

His knees gave out and hit the black tiles hard, his breath leaving him in a rush. He didn't feel the pain of his bones striking the floor. He couldn't feel anything over the agony tearing his heart to pieces and devouring his soul.

"Lucifer." Her voice was light in the darkness.

Warmth in the cold.

It curled around him and he foolishly clung to it as he shook, his strength flooding from him. Pathetic. He barked a mirthless laugh, one of self-reproach. Where was the proud King of Hell now?

Where was the male who had vowed to make everyone pay for what had happened to him, who had sat on his throne and ordered the deaths of thousands, who tormented and destroyed the souls of the sinful?

He pressed his left hand to his chest and clawed at it, feeling as if his own soul was the one being destroyed now.

He snarled an oath in the demon tongue, cursing the feelings that Erin had reawakened and Nina had restored to full strength.

He couldn't live with this heaviness on his chest, this crushing pressure of feeling the weight of his sins again.

"Lucifer?" Nina's soft fingers danced across his cheeks, her voice offering him comfort that made him want to reach out and pull her into his arms, to forget his pain by losing himself in her.

One hand lowered, coming to rest over the one he held pressed against his chest. Her fingers slipped between it and his body, stroking across his palm, and he stilled as she drew his hand towards her.

"Don't hurt yourself, Lucifer." The sound of his name softly falling from her lips only made the ache in his heart worsen.

Hell, he wanted to drown in her.

He slowly lifted his head and opened his eyes, stared at her where she knelt in front of him, a slight smile curving her shell-pink lips and her eyebrows furrowed, filling her tender gaze with concern.

Concern for him.

He'd had countless women, had used the power of his voice to sway them into looking at him with desire if they feared him or had accepted their natural attraction to him and used it to get what he had wanted from them, but he had never met a woman like Nina.

He had never found a female who looked at him with a mixture of passion and tenderness.

A combination he was coming to crave seeing in her steady gaze.

He had hidden himself from everyone, had shielded himself behind a façade to stop the world from seeing him for what he truly was, because he had feared they wouldn't understand.

Nina had seen beyond the veil though. He had shown her things that had tested her and she had accepted them, and he wanted to believe that if she saw the darkest part of him that she would understand and accept that too.

Even when he knew she wouldn't.

And that would crush him.

He bared his short fangs at that thought and shoved back against the feelings invading him.

Emotions were a weakness, one he had worked to eradicate for a reason. He tore his gaze away from her and ground his teeth as he fought to master his own mind, heart and body. He had no use for emotions. They were only a source of pain and suffering. He had shed them and they were no longer welcome. They weren't needed. He would purge them again. He would remove Nina from his sight, from his castle, and then he would return to the male he was now.

The master of the realm he had created.

The King of Hell.

The soft brush of her fingers across his right cheek undid him, his strength unravelling before he could fully gather it to shield himself against her. He couldn't stop himself from seeking her gaze.

He couldn't stop himself from leaning into her tender caress and stealing more from her.

He needed more.

He needed all of her.

He shot his hands out and snagged her waist, dragging her against him and drinking her gasp in a kiss as he crushed her lips with his. She responded instantly, her mouth opening for him and her tongue coming to brush his lips.

Lucifer snarled and deepened the kiss as he wrapped his arms around her waist and rose onto his knees, so she was pinned against his chest. She moaned and he shuddered from the sweet sound, a sudden desperation to draw another one from her filling him. He dropped his hands to her backside and got onto his feet, ripping another startled gasp from her soft lips, one that he devoured as he sought more from her.

Her hands clutched his shoulders, her fingertips pressing into his flesh in the most delicious way as he turned with her and pressed her against the vanity unit. He could feel the desperation flowing through her too, the hunger that she could no longer deny.

The passion neither of them could hold back anymore.

Lucifer set her down on the top of the black unit, prised her knees apart and slid between them. Hell, his already rock hard shaft kicked in his trousers as she pressed forwards, bringing them into contact. She was warm against him, teasing him with her heat and the thought of being inside her. He managed to kiss her for only a handful of seconds before the need to touch her become too fierce, hijacking his fragile sense of control and shattering it.

He grabbed the hem of her short skirt and shoved it upwards, tearing another moan from her as he continued to kiss her. Her nails scored his shoulders as she angled her head and kissed him harder, and it was his turn to gasp as she nipped at his lower lip and sucked on it.

Fuck.

He growled into her mouth, pushed his hands under her skirt and tugged at her stockings, swiftly pulling them down her legs. She wriggled, bringing her knees up between them, her eagerness only driving him on.

Driving him wild.

That realisation hit him with force, knocking him back a step, making him take a look at the woman who sat before him, frantically shoving her own tights down her legs and tossing them away from her.

A woman had never reacted to him the way she did.

A woman had never made him burn with need for her, driven him wild with a hunger to touch and taste her, to make love with her. A woman had never affected him the way Nina did.

He couldn't get enough of her.

He knew that.

No matter what he did. No matter how many times they made love. Not even if he had forever with her.

He would never get enough of her.

She lifted those stunning peridot eyes to meet his and a touch of colour stained her cheeks, the blush only luring him deeper under her spell. He brushed the backs of his fingers across her cheek, feeling the heat of her on his skin, and relished the way her eyelids fell to half-mast and she leaned into his touch.

She slowly lifted her eyelids and her gaze was wicked as it drifted over his bare chest, passion darkening it and commanding him to satisfy her. She wanted him, and he would give himself to her. He would ruin her to all other men, so she would never want another.

He would make her belong to him.

Her eyes followed his hands as he skimmed his palms up her silky bare thighs, her breathing coming quicker as he slid them under her skirt, pushing it further up, exposing her cream knickers. He slipped his fingers into the sides of them and eased them down. She pressed her hands to the counter on either side of her hips and raised herself so he could remove her underwear.

His own heart beat harder as he pulled them down, revealing a neat thatch of dark red curls.

His cock jerked hard against the confines of his trousers, aching with a need to be inside her and feel her wet heat gloving him.

He focused on pulling her knickers down her legs, his gaze slowly shifting upwards, over her hips and then her chest as he gradually came to kneel before her. She looked down at him, her hands still grasping the edges of the counter, her eyes dark with need. They were no longer soft though. No longer tender nor submissive.

A command filled them.

One that thrilled him.

She tipped her head back, her eyes still locked on his, and he knew with every fibre of his being what she desired.

And he would give it to her.

He tossed her knickers aside, ran his hands up her slender calves to her knees, and gently parted them, revealing her to him. She moaned and he groaned with her, the sight of her plush petals glistening with moisture and the smell of her desire almost doing him in. He wanted to taste her, needed it like a starving man needed sustenance. He would drink from her, would devour her, and take a piece of her into him. A piece he knew would only make him crave her even more.

He caught her hips and pulled her right to the edge of the counter, until she was close to his face. His gaze held hers and she issued that silent challenge again, one that demanded he satisfy her.

Lucifer kept his eyes on hers, unable to tear them away, hungry to see her reaction as he dipped his head towards her. The moment his tongue flicked out and over her tight bud, she tossed her head back and moaned. Her lips parted sweetly, her wild auburn hair falling back from her shoulders and neck, exposing them to him.

He groaned and licked her, softly at first, eliciting breathless gasps from his little female. As he pressed harder, each stroke of his tongue firmer than the last, her moans grew louder, filling the room and seeming to fill him too, satisfying him as he satisfied her.

He growled and she shuddered, as if that sound born of hunger and need had satisfied her too.

Thrilled her.

Lucifer couldn't hold back the possessive snarl that rumbled up his throat. He unleashed it as he licked her harder and delved lower, dragging her against his face and closing his eyes. He found her opening and thrust his tongue inside, and she jerked upwards, a sharp gasp leaving her before she sank back against him. He thrust again, mimicking sex, his thick cock throbbing with a need to be where his tongue was. She was tight and hot around him, tempting him into surrendering to that need to be inside her.

The soft rustle of material drew his gaze back up to her and he groaned as he swept back up to lick her tender nub, watching her as she unbuttoned her blouse and parted it. His pulse accelerated, his blood on fire as it rushed through his veins and he silently willed her to remove her clothing for him. He wanted to see her breasts. He wanted to devour their hard peaks as he made love with her.

She shirked her blouse, letting it fall behind her, and made fast work of her bra.

He had barely a glimpse of the dark pink buds of her nipples before she covered them. Tease. He swept his tongue harder over her clit, ripping another gasping moan from her, punishing her for being so wicked.

She punished him right back.

She took her nipples between her finger and thumb and rolled them, the look of bliss that crossed her face stopping him in his tracks and making him forget what he had been doing.

Hell.

He shot to his feet and kissed her hard, bruising her lips with his, unable to control himself as the image of her touching herself filled his mind. He braced his hands against the mirror behind her, his fingers splayed against the cold glass, trapping her between his arms. She moaned and slipped her hands between their bodies, capturing his hips and then drifting lower. Her fingernails lightly scraped his skin as she traced the waist of his trousers, tearing a moan from him as he tackled her tongue with his own, driving her back into submission.

She refused to go.

Her fingers made swift work of his button and zipper, and he shuddered and moaned, his arms shaking as he braced his weight on the mirror, when she cupped his hard cock and wrapped her fingers around the rigid length. She groaned, her kiss growing fiercer as she lazily stroked him. Her thumb brushed the head, smearing the evidence of his need into the softer skin.

He couldn't take it.

He growled at her, dropped one hand to her hip and the other to his cock, and pulled her towards him. She released him and leaned back, surrendering to him at last, and he stared down at his cock as she opened for him, parting her thighs wide to accommodate him. He ran the head of his length down her, groaning at the warm wetness and the promise of what was to come.

His gaze sought hers as he pressed inside her and he drank in the pleasure that flitted across her beautiful face. Her eyebrows furrowed, her lips parting on a whispered gasp, and her eyes closed as he eased into her. Inch by inch. She gloved him tightly, was so hot and wet that he trembled as he fought to stop himself from climaxing at just the feel of her around him.

His control shattered again as he reached the halfway point and he shoved deep into her, until he was fully seated, and could feel every inch of her and the way she trembled around him.

"Lucifer," she murmured and he obeyed that command.

He clutched her hip in one hand, braced himself against the mirror with the other, and slowly eased out of her before sliding back in. She moaned and tossed her head back, and he swooped on her throat, devouring it with wet kisses and nipping it as he thrust into her with long leisurely strokes. Every inch of him screamed for more, demanding he take her harder and faster, ordering him to find the pleasure he wanted with her.

He ignored that pounding need, because he needed this more.

He buried his face in her throat and drove into her, drinking every gasping moan that left her lips and savouring how she clutched his shoulders, as if she needed an anchor in this moment and he was that for her. He would be anything for her.

Everything.

He growled, screwed his eyes shut and increased the pace of his thrusts, his legs trembling as pleasure rolled through him. Her lips pressed against his shoulder, her kisses softer now, coaxing that gentler part of himself that he had forgotten existed but that he had found again in her arms.

She wrapped those arms around him, cradling him to her as he made love with her. He lowered both hands and held her to him, clutching her tightly as he thrust into her, losing himself as he found himself.

She moaned and her legs came up, sliding around his waist and her feet locking behind his backside. He shuddered and groaned as he slid deeper into her with each thrust and she tightened around him, her soft sighs pleading him for more.

More that he willingly gave to her.

He held her to him, crushing her against his chest as he thrust deeper, each stroke faster than the last. Her heart thundered against his, their pace matching as his breath sawed from him. Her rapid pants in his ear drove him on and he groaned as he gave himself over to desire again, to the pressing need beginning to fill him. He needed to feel her climax. He needed to hear her cry his name at the height of her pleasure.

Nina clung to him, her nails digging into his back and her feet pressing into his bottom, driving him forwards whenever he retreated. His wicked little female. She knew what she wanted and how to get it from him.

He grasped her hips and thrust faster, shallower strokes that struck as deep as he could go.

"More," she uttered and he shuddered, his knees shaking as he obeyed.

He grasped the back of her neck with his right hand and kissed her, bending her to his will as he took her, making her feel every inch of him as he withdrew until he was almost free of her before driving back into her. She cried into his mouth, the desperate sound laced with purest pleasure. He snarled and pumped into her, not relenting, driving her higher with each fierce thrust.

She tangled the fingers of her right hand in his hair, clutching it so tightly that it hurt, and grabbed his shoulder with her other hand, her kiss frantic as she began to tremble.

She tightened, her body flexing around his cock with each deep plunge of it into her.

"Nina," he groaned into her mouth and shoved into her.

"Lucifer!" She arched against him, thrusting her breasts against his bare chest, and tensed, every inch of her going rigid before she quivered around his cock, her thighs shaking against his hips with the force of her climax.

The feel of her milking his cock sent him careening over the edge with her and he shuddered and groaned, her name falling from his lips with each one as fire and lightning arced through him and he spilled himself inside her.

He sank against her and she cushioned him, her grip on him easing but not releasing him as she leaned back over the sink. His head came to rest on her shoulder and he sighed out his breath as he tried to bring himself down and settle his racing heart. She trembled around him, the aftershocks of her climax sending ripples of pleasure through him, echoes of his own.

Her left hand skimmed downwards and she was stroking the line of the thick ridge of scar tissue on his right shoulder before he realised what she was doing.

He tensed and she murmured softly, "I'm not going to ask about them."

Lucifer closed his eyes, sighed out his breath, and relaxed against her. Her fingers lightly stroked the scars and his wings itched for freedom. He held them at bay, fighting them as he absorbed with awe the comfort that she could give him with only a soft caress. There was tenderness in that touch that floored him, left him speechless and reeling. He had never realised he could feel so relaxed, so at peace while someone was holding him like this.

While his guard was down and he felt as if he had been stripped bare.

Made vulnerable.

Not by making love with her, but by that simple light touch that ran up and down his shoulder.

No one had ever touched him like this.

With love and understanding.

With hope in their heart.

For millennia, he had known only the despair of others. He had relished their fear, their desperation and their pain. He had savoured their defeat.

Now he relished Nina's affection, her tenderness and the care she showed to him. He savoured her hope, even when he knew she would never understand. She believed that she would.

She wouldn't, and he couldn't blame her. All he could do was steal every drop of her growing affection for him and hope it was enough to keep him going if she ever discovered the things about him he was beginning to want to hide from her forever.

He knew that she wouldn't ask about the scars on his back. She would keep that promise until he was ready to tell her.

He wasn't sure he would ever be ready.

Because he feared that if she knew what he was, who he was, that she would leave him.

She would take this away from him.

He had found heaven again in her arms.

He had found his home in her.

CHAPTER 11

Nina had the feeling she had made a terrible mistake by sleeping with Lucifer, but she couldn't bring herself to regret it. She ran her fingers through the short dewy grass, lost in the feel of the blades tickling her palms as she stared at the mountains opposite her. Time slipped through her fingers as easily as the blades as she thought about the man in the fortress at her back and watched the sunlight playing on the river.

Lucifer had been reluctant to leave her this morning after they had dragged themselves out of bed and eaten breakfast together. She had sensed his need to go somewhere, and had mentioned that she wanted to spend more time in the valley. His smile had been charming, a little boyish but touched with pride that had brought out her own smile. She had pleased him by desiring to visit this place of his creation.

He had made her feel it really was a place he had constructed and therefore controlled when he had walked her down the long black tunnel and opened the door for her.

It had still been night, and she had enjoyed the stars for a time with him, her standing in the valley but him inside the tunnel.

Their hands linked through the barrier that prevented him from joining her.

When he had announced that he needed to leave her but that she would be safe in the valley, she had asked him to change night back into day. While she loved the beauty of the valley at night and the stars that filled the heavens, she couldn't stop herself from thinking about the sensation she'd had in the woods, the feeling that something was in the darkness watching her.

Lucifer had responded by drawing her into the tunnel with him, lifting their joined hands to his lips and pressing a kiss to hers. His eyes had sworn a promise to her that no one would ever hurt her, that she had no reason to fear because he was there for her. It had melted her, and she had wanted to hold that promise to her chest and take it into her heart, but a piece of her still feared the darkness.

So Lucifer had given her light.

She wrapped her arms around her blue jeans-clad legs as she thought about how much his hand had shaken against hers while he had been changing the time of day for her, bringing about a rapid moonset and sunrise. It had been beautiful.

And she had thanked him with a kiss.

Nina brushed her fingers across her lower lip. They still tingled from the force of his kiss.

A kiss that had been laced with desperation and need that had made her want to ask him what he was thinking about, but he had set her into the light and had turned away before she could find the courage to voice that question.

She had been thinking about it ever since.

That and the man who had kidnapped her and had come back for her.

She leaned forwards, rested her chin on her knees and sighed as she idly stroked the sleeves of the soft cream cashmere sweater she wore.

Her eyes scanned the mountains and drifted lower, tracking down to the woods and charting a path through them. Was it possible to climb the mountains and see beyond the barrier surrounding the valley?

She pushed that thought aside, shunning it.

She wasn't sure whether she really wanted to see beyond this beautiful place. She wasn't sure she wanted to shatter the illusion of peace she felt here. She knew that if all that surrounded the valley and castle was black as it had been when she had found the limit of the valley, she would freak out and would have another panic attack.

She had never been one for burying her head in the sand, but right now she wanted to feel safe.

She wanted to feel that nothing would happen to her here.

She wasn't in danger.

Her thoughts turned to the man again, the one Lucifer had fought to keep her safe.

He must have been sent by her ex-husband.

Nina couldn't think of anyone else who would want to hurt her, or abduct her.

She had tried to leave her past behind her, had tried to shut out the pain he had inflicted on her, the agony that he had put her through, and she had been managing it until he had contacted her out of the blue.

All of the hurt had come flooding back on receiving a phone call from him and hearing his voice once again.

She had almost broken down in the middle of the shopping mall but had managed to make it to a quiet corner where she had pressed her back to the cool fake stone wall and slid down it to sit on the floor.

She squeezed her eyes shut against the tears that threatened to fill them and cursed his name in her head.

She had given him everything. Six years of her life. Her love. Her loyalty.

Her heart.

She had stood by him during the inquiries into his business and his empire. She had turned a blind eye to the shady dealings he had done with dangerous characters to further that empire, turning himself into a powerful figure, one who was both respected and feared. She had done everything for him.

How had he repaid her?

He had left her for another woman when he had realised that she couldn't get pregnant.

God, she had wanted children and had wanted to give him what he had desired, but she hadn't been able to and it had killed her. She had thought that he would stand by her, and he had betrayed her.

He had destroyed her.

She had heard through the grapevine that he had married again.

But it had been a surprise when he had called to ask her to meet him, had sounded so desperate to see her again and had told her that his wife had left him, taking half of his fortune and their children with her.

Nina had foolishly spoken to him, and even stupidly met with him at a café.

Part of her had wanted him to see that she was happy without him, that she didn't need him and she had moved on. She had wanted him to see that her life was going well when his had gone to hell. She had wanted him to suffer as she had.

She hadn't expected him to reach across the table in the middle of their conversation, take hold of her hand and announce that he wanted to get back together with her.

It had sent her reeling, throwing her for a moment and knocking her off balance, until he had added that he had children now and they could be together again.

That had stung.

No.

That had shoved a hot needle through her heart.

He had found what he had wanted with someone else and now he wanted to get back together with her, because he didn't need to have any more children.

He had made her feel as if she was playing second fiddle all over again. A person with a piece missing, one that made her less valuable than others.

Nina had left without giving him an answer, but he had phoned her repeatedly and left messages. Each message had turned more desperate, until the last one she had received just the day before the man had kidnapped her.

That one had sounded threatening to her.

Was it really possible that he had sent the man?

Yes. She knew that in her heart. All those years ago, when they had first met, he had pursued her. He had persisted and never relented. He had done everything to win her.

She felt certain that he would do everything in his power to win her back too.

Even go as far as having her kidnapped in order to make her talk to him again.

She needed to speak with Lucifer and warn him about her ex-husband. She hated talking about her past, had bottled it up and kept it to herself, but Lucifer needed to know what he had gotten himself into by helping her.

He deserved to know.

Nina picked herself up off the grass, dusted the damp backside of her jeans down, and took one last look at the valley. She breathed deep of the crisp cool air, finding a sense of peace, the strength to do what was right and open her heart and reveal her past to Lucifer.

She finally wanted to share the burden with someone.

She turned and entered the tunnel, picked up the flaming torch that waited there, and began walking up the sloping path. The air grew colder the further she moved from the valley, but it no longer chilled her. She felt warmed inside, filled with courage and hope, heated by the thought of finally speaking with someone about what had happened to her.

Finally letting someone back inside.

She reached the apartment and disposed of the torch in the fireplace before approaching the door to the corridor. She hesitated only a second before grasping the handle and pulling the door open. The black-walled hallway was empty in both directions. She recalled that Lucifer had been walking towards the left end of it when she had stopped him last night. Was his bedroom that way?

She stepped out into the hallway and walked along it, opening the door to each room she passed to check whether Lucifer was inside.

She had reached the fifth door when footsteps echoed from ahead of her. Lucifer.

Nina picked up the pace, a smile rising onto her lips as she thought about seeing him again.

That smile died when a brunet male rounded the corner ahead of her. He carried a silver tray with a domed cover on it, and she stared at the reflection in it, unable to believe her eyes, and then glanced at the man.

He looked perfectly normal as he stood before her, dressed in a black suit similar to the one Lucifer wore.

She looked back down at the cloche.

Slowly shook her head.

In the reflection on it, he wore something that resembled black armour over his broad chest, his arms left bare above the elbow, but encased in black guards around his forearms.

Nina backed off a step and flicked another glance at the man.

A thousand hot needles pierced her skull and she grunted as she clutched it, pressing her hands hard against her temples. Tears filled her eyes as she fought to breathe, but she gave up when the suit the man wore disappeared and he stood before her dressed in armour that covered his chest, hips, shins and forearms. What the heck?

She cried out as the pain in her head grew more intense and her eyes widened in horror as huge crimson wings sprouted from the man's back.

Like an angel.

The hallway twirled around her and she staggered to her right, hit the wall there and crashed to the ground. Images flashed through her mind, whirling together and then separating to reveal them. Her stomach turned as she caught individual ones long enough to make sense of them. The fortress. Lucifer's powers. The angel before her. His eyes burned red.

As red as Lucifer's had.

Fangs.

Shadow wings.

A terrible power that she couldn't comprehend.

The black lands beyond the barrier.

How charming and dangerous he seemed.

Nina clutched her stomach as sickness brewed in it, dread pooling there as she realised who he was and where she was. She had to escape. Her skin prickled, fiercest down the line of her spine, and an urgent needed blasted through her, overpowering the quieter voice that pressed her to find Lucifer and discover what was happening.

She wanted to know, and this was her chance, but she was afraid.

She feared everything she felt for him, everything she had felt while she had been with him, had been a lie.

That word echoed in her head, hissed on repeat, urging her onto her feet. Lies. He had lied to her. She had to get away. She had to flee.

No, she didn't want to run.

The urge grew stronger, overwhelming her, and she was running before she knew it, bolting down the corridor in a blind dash for freedom.

Freedom from what?

Her heart screamed that Lucifer would never hurt her. He had protected her. He had taken care of her.

Her head shrieked at her to keep running. Lies. All of it. Lucifer was the prince of lies. The sower of discord.

The Devil.

She grunted and held her head harder as she saw flashes of him with great black wings and she zoomed around him, coming to see his back.

Those wings sprouted from the place where she knew scars to be.

He was a liar. He was using her. She had to escape now, before he returned.

Before it was too late.

That need drove her to keep running, even as her heart tried to rebel and make her stop. Whenever she thought about stopping, the pain in her head grew stronger, turning her thoughts hazy and allowing more images to invade her mind. Every charming smile Lucifer had given her. Every time he had asked her about the man who had taken her. Every moment when he had been watching her with coldness in his eyes.

They all crashed together until she saw one final image.

Lucifer standing before her while she struggled to remember the man who had kidnapped her.

And with blinding clarity she knew that he had pushed her in that moment, he had driven her to remember.

He had used his powers against her.

Nina screamed and sprinted down the stairs in the towering entrance hall. The moment she hit the ground floor, she broke right, heading for the enormous twin doors. They opened for her and she rushed through them, and skidded to a halt, her breath leaving her in a gasp.

Black spires of rock rose in a curve around an obsidian courtyard under a pitch-dark sky. Beyond those spires, cragged grim land reigned, and in the distance rose a plateau. Light shone there, pure and warm.

Light that drew her towards it and filled her with a desperate need to reach it, because every instinct she possessed said that she would escape this hell if she made it there.

Nina ran towards it, her sneakers pounding the smooth pavement.

Screams rose around her, garbled cries that turned her stomach and chilled her to her bones. She kept running, pushing herself beyond her limit, unable to heed the part of her that told her to slow down and even stop. She had to keep running. Lucifer was a liar.

The Devil.

A heartless, merciless, and cold being.

It had all been a lie.

Nina's head turned foggy and she nodded, agreeing with everything that was running through her mind, even when a piece of her screamed not to listen. She scaled the rocks at the opposite end of the courtyard to the fortress, clambered between two of the gigantic spires, and lost her footing. She slid down the slope on the other side, hit the ground hard and rolled, grunting as the small stones and rocks lashed at her.

The air was too thick to breathe, the stench making her gag as she pushed herself up and wearily found her feet. She had to keep running.

Her eyes sought the light again.

She had to reach there.

It called to her.

It filled her heart with sweet promises and she was powerless to ignore them.

Nina kept running, her mind growing numb but her body seemingly alive, able to function without her brain working it. Her feet carried her straight towards a winding path that led up to the plateau without her even noticing it. Her eyes were fixed on the light above her, never straying from it. She couldn't bring herself to look away from it. She had to keep looking at it.

She had to reach it.

Her breath sawed from her burning lungs as she finally reached the plateau and the bright golden light.

It was so strong that it stung her eyes and blinded her, and she raised her hand to shield them.

"You do not belong here." A soft melodious male voice curled around her and the light faded enough that she could lower her hand and seek the owner of it.

A man stood before her, his white hair tied in a ponytail and his blue eyes filled with warmth that beckoned her to him.

An angel.

White wings furled against his back and he held his hand out to her.

"I will take you home."

Nina reached for him and, despite the distance that was between them, her hand slipped into his as if he had been standing only inches from her.

She looked up at his handsome face and blinked slowly.

This was wrong.

She had to speak with Lucifer. She didn't want to leave him.

The angel's eyes brightened, darker flakes swirling among the paler blue, and her head felt heavy again.

"Come with me."

She nodded and stepped closer to him when he drew his arm back. He wrapped his other arm around her and she looked up into his eyes, drifting in them among the incredible blue, hazy from head to toe.

"I will see to it that you are safe and that the vile creature has not harmed you, and can never harm you again."

Nina frowned at that, something buried deep inside her warning her that she wasn't safe with this man, she was only safe with Lucifer. That fleeting feeling melted away as the man spread his beautiful wings and beat them. She had to go with him.

"The Devil is a cruel and vicious beast. He has used you ill. He has spread his lies like poison through you. You will be safe now."

Nina nodded. She would be safe.

The light engulfed them and when it receded, she found herself standing in the middle of her small London apartment. The heaviness in her mind began to lift, the fog parting, and she gently broke free of the angel's arms. She staggered back a few steps, placing some distance between them, and looked around her and then at him.

"Remain here. You will be safe in this place. The Devil will no longer be able to reach you." The angel closed the distance between them and brushed his fingers across her cheek, and Nina shuddered and withdrew, a cold sensation running through her, born of his touch. He smiled. "The Devil will no longer be able to hurt you."

But he hadn't hurt her.

He had been kind, tender even, and had taken care of her.

The angel locked eyes with her again and her head hurt, flashes of Lucifer with cold eyes filling it.

She pushed back against them and looked at the angel.

There was something familiar about him, something that triggered a hazy sense that she shouldn't trust him. She couldn't trust anyone. Everyone had toyed with her to a degree. Lucifer.

The angels.

Her eyes widened.

The man who had taken her had been an angel.

Nina's knees gave out and she hit the wooden floor with a crack.

The angel went to crouch and she held her hands out, warning him away.

"I just need to rest," she muttered to his knees. "I need to sleep. If you don't mind?"

She lifted her eyes to meet his and he nodded, his ponytail shifting with it.

Long hair.

Dread pooled in her stomach again, heavier this time, sickening her.

She didn't remember how she had ended up in Hell, but something warned her that this man had been involved. He hadn't just happened to be on that plateau either, with that beam of light that had lured her to it. He had been waiting for her.

If Lucifer had indeed played her, manipulated her mind and used her, then this angel had done infinitely worse to her.

He had stolen her from her world, dumped her with the Devil, and had then lured her back to him. Why?

He towered over her, his eyes colder now that she was afraid of him and was regaining her senses. His white wings rose above his broad shoulders, his black breastplate shifting with each steady breath he drew. She felt colder the longer she looked up at him, fear bubbling up inside her. She had to make him leave.

"If you don't mind?" she said again, putting more force into her words this time.

The angel regarded her for a few long seconds in which her heart raced and her palms sweated, her fear growing stronger until she could scarcely breathe, and then nodded.

He backed off a step and bright light burst into the room, blinding her. When her vision came back, he was gone.

Relief crashed over her and she sank forwards, curling into a ball.

How was it that she had felt threatened and in danger around an angel, yet she had felt safe with Lucifer?

Nina rolled onto her side and hugged her knees.

She wasn't sure what was happening, or whether she had simply gone insane, and she wasn't sure that she would ever know, because deep in her heart she knew that only one man could give her the answers to her questions.

Nina pressed her hand to the floor, reaching down through the levels of the building and beyond, to where she imagined Hell to be.

A man she felt certain she would never see again.

The Devil.

CHAPTER 12

Lucifer lifted his head and scoured the horizon as a sensation of power ran through him. His golden gaze halted on the plateau and the bright shaft of light illuminating Hell there.

Mihail.

His eyes darted to his fortress and darkness swallowed the land around him before separating to reveal the courtyard and the twin doors towering before him.

They were open.

His heart lurched in his chest and he sprinted into the building, his power reaching outwards, stretching invisible fingers through the castle as he searched for Nina.

A cold shiver ran down his spine and he turned back towards the door in time to see the light on the plateau stutter and die.

Nina.

His breath left him in a rush and he could only stare at the dark plateau, ice stealing through his veins as his heart throbbed madly behind his breast.

"No," he uttered and shook his head, refusing to believe that she had left him.

He growled and whirled back to face the vestibule and the floating staircases. Black shadows streamed from his fingers as he raised his hands and ribbons of darkness furled outwards, splitting and multiplying as they scoured the castle. Nina was still here. She wouldn't have left him.

He had made sure of that. He had taken steps to ensure she wouldn't discover where she was. The main doors had been locked to her. His men under orders to conceal their true appearance should she venture from her room.

"No," he snarled as his shadows reached the top of the tallest of the towers and he realised she wasn't anywhere within the fortress.

The valley.

Lucifer teleported to her room and didn't hesitate. He ran straight to the corridor that would take him to the valley and sprinted down it, his shoes loud on the cobbled floor and his heightened vision revealing the black tunnel to him without need for light to guide him.

He didn't stop running until he hit the invisible barrier at the end.

He pressed his palms to it and tried to reach through it with his shadows, but the light drove them back, the boundaries of his imprisonment stopping them from seeking Nina.

"Nina!" Lucifer banged his fists against the barrier, sure that she would hear him if she was in the valley.

He bellowed her name at the top of his lungs until he was hoarse and the sky in the valley had turned black, heavy clouds rolling in to pelt the land with hail the size of his clenched fists. Lightning forked the sky and he clawed at the barrier, his long black nails raking down it as he breathed hard. The river surged, the boiling water crashing over the wooden bridge and carrying it away.

Snow cracked on the mountaintops with a boom and tumbled downwards, picking up speed as it thundered towards the valley. The air filled with the groans and snapping of the trees as the avalanche ploughed through them, ripping them from the hillside.

Lucifer snarled and his wings burst from his back, his short obsidian horns emerging and protruding through his black hair as they grew, flaring forwards from behind his ears to beyond his temples.

He bared his fangs as his eyes blazed crimson and lightning struck the highest peak.

Stone exploded and rained down on the valley, huge chunks of it carving up the earth and the grass. A massive boulder bounced off the peak of the hill and hit the fortress, shaking the walls.

"Nina," Lucifer whispered and pressed his palms to the barrier, his heart on fire and burning with a need to see her.

He needed her back.

He closed his eyes, lowered his head and teleported back to the entrance hall of the fortress.

He wasn't alone.

Lucifer lifted his head and pinned deadly crimson eyes on the wretched creature standing opposite him.

One of his men.

The larger male shifted foot-to-foot, his skin paling as he looked at Lucifer. Afraid.

Not because he was witnessing a side of Lucifer that he worked hard to keep hidden—his true appearance.

The male feared because he knew why Lucifer was angry.

He knew Nina was gone.

Lucifer roared at him, every single one of his teeth sharpening into vicious points. The male stumbled backwards, hit the wall near the door rather than the space he had clearly aimed for in an attempt to flee, and quickly held his hands up.

"I did nothing wrong, Master." The male fell to his knees and lowered his head.

The bastard should beg for his life.

Lucifer raised his hand, ready to strike him down and send him back to Heaven for what he had done. He had frightened Nina away. Lucifer knew it. The imbecile had been careless and she had seen him for what he was.

"I was bringing her food as you requested, Master," the male stammered into his knees and then dared to raise his head and look directly at him. Lucifer sneered and flexed his fingers, and the male flinched away and rushed out, "My wings were concealed! I didn't break the rules. I swear it. When she saw me, she became pained. She had some sort of episode and I tried to help her. I tried to stop her."

Lucifer lowered his hand on hearing that and the male whimpered, curling into himself, obviously anticipating death.

He stared at the male, sifting through his memories until he found the one he wanted.

Lucifer flexed his clawed fingers. He hadn't lied. The male had hidden himself, using a glamour to alter his appearance, and his wings had not been out.

Nina had seen through the spell somehow.

There was only one way that was possible.

Mihail had done something to her that Lucifer had failed to detect. He had altered her memories and implanted something in her, something that had been triggered on seeing someone other than Lucifer, allowing her to witness the Hell's angel in his true appearance and granting her the ability to leave the fortress.

Lucifer still wasn't sure what her orders had been, but he knew one thing.

He couldn't let her go.

He needed her back.

The space she had filled inside his chest was already hollowing out again, turning blacker than before, and now he didn't want to return to how things had been. He didn't want to be without her, even when he knew that he didn't deserve her.

Even when he felt certain she could never love a monster like him.

Lucifer slowly walked towards the Hell's angel, who cowered as he approached, and then beyond him, out onto the steps of his fortress.

He stared across the distance to the plateau, rage burning in his heart as his shadow wings fluttered from his back, itching for him to take flight and decimate the forces of Heaven who stood guard there.

But his enemy was not here.

Mihail was gone, and had taken Nina with him.

Lucifer had failed to protect her from the angel.

He tipped his head back and looked at the cragged ceiling of Hell.

But he wouldn't fail to take her back.

His gaze darted from one spot to another across the black vault above him, easily leaping from each invisible seal to the next. Need filled him, a terrible urge to break every one of the seals that kept him locked in Hell. He growled through his sharp teeth and reined in that desire. It would only spark Heaven into sending angels to stop him, and even if they didn't, it wouldn't work. It wouldn't bring him what he desired.

By breaking every seal, he would free himself but he would also end the world.

As little as people thought of him, he wasn't a heartless bastard.

He didn't want to bring about the end of this planet.

He loved his realm as it was, in one piece, and himself as he was, alive.

If he was to reach Nina, he would require a more covert way of crossing from his realm and into the mortal one.

There was only one way.

Lucifer closed his eyes and reached out to his daughter, easily locating her on her island paradise.

"Daughter, come to me," he whispered the words into her mind, keeping his voice calm and even so she couldn't detect the turbulent emotions churning inside him—the desperation to have her standing before him in Hell, the urgent need to see Nina again and ensure she was safe, and the fear that he would be unable to make either of those things happen.

What the fuck do you want?

His daughter had a little too much of his sassiness and viciousness at times.

"I require you…" Lucifer grimaced, swallowed his pride, and huffed. "I need your assistance."

Silence.

Holy fuck. Did you just say what I thought you did?

Lucifer snarled at her. She laughed in his head.

No need to get grumpy, Pops. What's the deal? You got a pest problem?

He smiled at that. His daughter viewed angels with the same disdain as he did after all they had done to her, her maggot of a husband, and her son, and those she deemed family.

The concern that edged her voice in her last question told him that she considered him part of the latter, despite her best efforts to hold him at a distance and hate him.

"Come to me and I will tell you."

Silence again.

She wasn't going to fall for it. The darkness inside him pushed, roaring to the surface and trying to break free. He contained it, unwilling to let her sense it in him or those who were in the vicinity see how upset he was. He refused to surrender to the black voice in his heart that pressed him to do whatever it took, born of his desperate need of Nina, because he feared that if he did, he would break the seals and destroy all three realms.

"Daughter," he said.

"What?" she snapped.

Not in his head.

Lucifer opened his eyes and fixed them on Erin where she stood a few metres from him, on the lower section of the courtyard, her hands planted on her hips over her short black summer dress and her golden eyes filled with irritation.

"So where's this invasion?" She looked around her, causing her short black bob to sway with the motion, the sense of anger and annoyance flowing from her growing in strength as she realised that there was no invasion.

He had to act quickly before his opportunity teleported right back beyond his reach.

An unfamiliar sensation squirmed in his stomach.

Guilt.

Before it had a chance to overpower him, he teleported in front of Erin and pressed his palm to her forehead. Wide golden eyes leaped up to meet his.

"I am sorry," he whispered and they only grew wider. "I need to borrow you as a vessel."

Fire blazed through him and he cried out in time with Erin. Black lightning zinged through his bones, crackled through the link between his palm and her brow, and then consumed him. The darkness faded and he opened his eyes.

He stared right back at himself through wide eyes.

"What the fucking hell?" His body snarled the words in his voice and turned on the spot, horror crossing his face.

Mortified was not a strong enough word to cover how Lucifer felt, especially when his body turned back to glare at him, his eyes glowing crimson as he snarled and his black horns flaring further forwards like twin dangerous daggers.

"What the fucking hell, indeed," Lucifer muttered and covered his hand with his mouth when his words came out in Erin's voice.

He hadn't anticipated that she would swap places with him too, occupying his body. He had thought that she would remain in her own body, her soul subdued by the strength of his.

"You took things too far this time, you bastard!" His body went from glaring at him to looking down at itself. "Oh, God, this is wrong. So... so... wrong."

Lucifer roared on hearing that word and lashed out. His arm moved ridiculously slowly, feeling sluggish and weak, and he stopped before he was even close to hitting himself across the face. Nothing seemed quite right.

He looked down at himself and his eyebrows shot up. He should have considered that he really would be inside Erin's body. She was right.

It felt wrong.

So, so wrong.

He shuddered and considered switching back with her, but Nina popped into his head. His beautiful Nina. He had to see her again and explain. He needed to know that she was safe.

"I am sorry." He was heading for the world record on the number of times he had apologised in one day but Erin looked as if she was considering grievous bodily harm and it was his body that she was occupying. "I will explain when I return."

"When you return?" she screamed in his voice and lurched forwards, towards him. "What the fuck? Don't you bloody dare!"

She snagged his arm before he could teleport to London, and he could only stare at her as he remained where he was rather than disappearing from her grasp. She had grown more powerful than he had ever expected, because no matter what he tried, he couldn't teleport while she was holding him. Or perhaps it was because she occupied his body, and he hers. It was weak, and he could feel it inhibiting his powers, dampening them to a degree. It would have irritated him if he hadn't been about to venture to the mortal realm, where his powers normally caused havoc even when he tried to contain them. With Erin's weaker body inhibiting them, there was a chance he could reach Nina without causing mass destruction.

If he could convince Erin to let him go that was.

He looked down at the hand on his slender bare arm and realised she wouldn't release him unless he did things her way.

He would have to explain things to her now, but it was going to be the short version of events. He wasn't sure where Mihail had taken Nina, but he needed to find her before something happened to her. There was every chance that Heaven would order her death if she had already fulfilled whatever purpose they had given her.

He couldn't let that happen.

"Mihail left a mortal female in my courtyard and I believe she was meant as bait."

His body raised an eyebrow at him. "Why?"

Lucifer wished that he had an answer to that question. "I do not know."

His body folded his arms and frowned, a very unlike him huff leaving his lips. "Did you do anything with this woman?"

The look in his golden eyes said that Erin was thinking badly of him, and that she believed that he had mistreated the female. He hadn't, but her question did make him realise something.

Something that chilled him to the depths of his soul and ignited a fear that he knew why Mihail had brought the woman, and why he had taken her from Lucifer.

Lucifer had played his part.

And the angel had played him well.

But he wouldn't get away with it.

Lucifer wouldn't allow Heaven to get their hands on his unborn child.

It explained why Mihail had returned to Hell, only to leave again when Lucifer had attempted to destroy him and had almost destroyed himself in the process. Mihail had believed that Nina had been with him long enough to be seduced by him. The angel must have had a way of discovering whether she had slept with him or not, and had left her in Hell when he had realised that Lucifer hadn't seduced her.

Because he hadn't wanted to seduce her.

Because she was more to him than a mere conquest.

He clenched his fists, Erin's longer nails biting into his palms, and stared at his body, trying to shake the other fear that grew inside him.

Fear that Nina had played him too.

What if it had all been an act and she had been in league with Heaven and their plans?

The darkness in his heart exploded as those words rang in his mind, filling his chest and bleeding through his veins. It seeped from his fingers and lashed at the black ground around him, snapping and cracking as it struck like lightning, sending shards of rock flying in all directions.

He gritted his sharpening teeth and snarled, his eyes blazing crimson and a red veil descending.

Poisonous words whispered in his head, driving him onwards, until the darkness had consumed him and he could think only of seeking out the mortal female and making her pay for what she had done to him.

She had betrayed him. Played him.

For the first time in millennia, he had trusted someone again and they had turned on him.

His chest ached, the fragile organ that he had fought to protect for centuries shattering within his breast.

His body reached for him, the compassion in his golden eyes only worsening his need for violence, his urge to lash out at everyone and everything around him until he was so exhausted that he was numb to the agony writhing inside him like a living thing.

Devouring him.

He tore his arm free from Erin's grip.

"You dare disappear with my damned—"

Lucifer teleported before she could finish, reappearing on a rooftop in London. It had changed dramatically since the last time he had set foot in the mortal realm, but he wasn't here to sightsee. He was here on business.

Somewhere in this city was a female, a viper that had poisoned him with emotions and then used them against him to get what she wanted.

He threw his head back and roared, the sound more beast than the feminine body he occupied, and shadows streamed from him to blanket the city, driving it into darkness as they devoured the light. Shrieks rose from the streets far below him, a cacophony of fearful cries that only delighted him. He grinned as he sensed their fear, tasted their despair, and struggled to focus on his target.

Nina.

Just the sound of her name in his head was enough to have him moving.

He spread his shadow wings and beat them hard, following his ribbons of darkness as they homed in on the mortal female.

His grin widened as they found her.

Alone.

The angel had been a fool to leave her unguarded.

CHAPTER 13

Lucifer teleported to a small terraced Victorian house in a quiet street, landing outside under a lamp that glowed orange. It flickered, crackled and exploded. Along the street in both directions, the other lamps did the same, causing darkness to race outwards with him at its epicentre.

He stared at the only light remaining in the street.

The light in the white sash window above him.

He growled and teleported inside the room.

Nina gasped and whirled to face him, her hand coming up fast in a silver flash. A knife. She stared at him in silence, her shock echoing through him. She stood in the middle of a group of beige couches in the centre of a cream drawing room, her back to an open door that revealed a tiny kitchen. A flicker of curiosity bolted through him. Why did she have a knife when she was far from the kitchen? Did she feel she needed protection?

That tempered his anger a little, making it fade a touch as a need to ensure she felt safe raced through him. Before that need could take hold, the darkness within him surged back to the fore, reminding him why he had come. He hadn't come here to protect her. He had come to make sure she knew the full extent of his wrath.

The ground trembled with it, sending her staggering back a few steps and struggling to retain her balance.

Fear washed across her face.

"Who the hell are you?" she snapped and brandished the knife.

It seemed the little mortal had already forgotten just who she had betrayed.

He stepped forwards and the awkward jiggling of his body dragged his focus downwards. To breasts and flared hips. Perhaps she hadn't forgotten who she had pissed off, but he had definitely forgotten that he wasn't himself.

The knife shook in her hand. "If you're with those angels… you can leave me the hell alone too. I'm warning you. Get out."

Lucifer canted his head, his short black bob brushing his neck in an irritating fashion.

She was trying to protect herself from the angels? Had she fought Mihail and that was the reason the angel had left her unguarded? Had he been wrong about her?

"I am not with the angels." He held his hand out to her, slender and feminine, tipped with long black nails. This would have been so much easier if he had his own damned body. Nina regarded it with cold eyes that burned in their depths, lending her a defiant and dangerous air that he found too damn alluring. "You know me."

"I don't know. I don't know what the fuck is going on anymore. One moment I'm with this great guy and the next I'm feeling like an extra in a zombie movie and I don't know what the heck my body was doing, but it wasn't doing what my mind told it to do. There was an angel, and I swear to God that—"

Lucifer roared at her, his eyes blazing crimson, and she paled and tensed. Blinked.

"Who are you?" she whispered but he wasn't sure how to answer that.

He wasn't sure he could think to explain it, because he was still stuck on what she had said when she had been babbling.

This great guy.

Him?

It didn't really seem plausible, but he had been the only male with her during her entire stay, and he had shared things with her that he had never shown to anyone. He had felt close to her in that time, and the hurt surfacing in her eyes and in her feelings said that he wasn't the only one who felt betrayed.

He stared into her peridot eyes, seeing the pain in them and the suffering, the agony that he felt in his heart.

"Nina," he murmured and reached for her, wanting to pull her into his arms and comfort her, needing to feel that she was still the woman he had fallen in love with and that she hadn't betrayed him.

Just as he hadn't betrayed her.

They had both been played.

"How do you know my name?" She shoved the knife towards him and he kept his distance, aware that if he harmed Erin's body, he would never hear the end of it.

He was never going to hear the end of it as it was.

"Because… I am Lucifer."

Her jaw dropped.

She rallied and shook her head. "No. I think I remember what he looked like. If that was even what he really looked like. He's a liar, right? He manipulates people and makes them do stuff. He made me—"

"No," he interjected and stepped towards her, deciding to close the distance a little at a time so he didn't scare her. "I never seduced you, Nina. I never used you. Whatever Mihail told you, it was a lie. He was the liar."

"Mihail?" she whispered, a distant look in her eyes, and then dropped the knife and clutched her head.

Her whimper tore at him and he couldn't stop himself from reaching for her, catching her arms and pulling her into the safety of his. She curled into him, shaking like a leaf, and he stroked her back and pressed a kiss to her ear when he had wanted to kiss the top of her head. Erin was too damned short too.

"I have you now. I will never allow anyone to hurt you. I swear that, Nina." He went to kiss her again and she jerked out of his arms, shoved him in the chest and pushed him away.

Lucifer gritted his teeth and rubbed his chest. Damn, that had hurt. Female bodies were strange. They experienced pain in places he normally didn't. They were weak.

The ground rocked again, and he couldn't curse the weakness of Erin's body. It was the only thing stopping that gentle trembling from becoming a devastating quake that would tear everything asunder, destroying the city.

"I told you, I don't know who you are." She clutched the sides of her head, her face screwing up, and then glared at him. "Leave."

"No." He wasn't leaving without her. He was staying where he was until she believed him and heard him out. He had to convince her that while his body was feminine, he was the man she knew inside.

How?

He didn't have much time. By now, Heaven would know he had escaped his containment and angels would be coming. Mihail would be among them, and he wasn't strong enough to fight the bastard and keep Nina safe, not in this body. He had to get her back to Hell. He smiled as it hit him.

"I can prove to you that I am Lucifer. I can tell you things that only you would know."

She stooped, scooped up the knife and scowled at him. "I highly doubt that."

"I made a valley, and I took you there when you were unwell. I wanted to make you feel at home." He drew down a deep breath and sighed it out when she looked sceptical still. This had to work, even when he knew it was only the first step. Even if he convinced her that he was who he said he was, it didn't mean she would return to Hell with him. "You complained about how static it was, and I said that it had changed you."

Her eyes slowly began to widen.

It was working.

"If you're Lucifer, then tell me what you said to me when I asked if it could grow dark?" she said and stared deep into his eyes.

He nodded. "Why would you desire to see the darkness?"

She looked away from him, beyond him to the window, her green eyes gaining a distant look. "At the time, I thought it was strange that I wanted to see it too. I thought about it a lot after that, and I realised that it was because you seemed to belong in the darkness. Now I guess I understand why that is."

You.

She was beginning to believe him.

"Nina," he whispered and she frowned at him.

He knew it sounded odd, that his voice was whiny and female, but he couldn't stop himself from saying her name. Hell help him, but he would kiss her if she allowed it.

"You really expect me to believe you're the Devil?" She looked him over, a confused crinkle to her brow.

He remained still when she closed the distance between them and shook her head, her gaze skimming up and down.

"I do not expect you to believe it, because I know you already feel it in your heart, Nina. We share a connection, one that runs as deep as blood, forged in that cramped bathroom. I did not seduce you, Nina." He lifted his hand and brushed his knuckles across her cheek. "You seduced me."

Her wide eyes halted on his, realisation shining in them together with something else, and she covered her mouth.

"Oh, God, you're a cross-dresser too."

Lucifer growled at her, unable to stop himself on hearing that word, and she didn't flinch away this time. She remained where she was, no trace of fear in her scent as she stared at him in disbelief. He struggled to rein in his anger again, wondering at the same time whether she would ever learn to not use that word around him. When he had managed to calm himself, he found her standing closer to him.

Prodding his breasts.

"They feel so real."

Lucifer gently slapped her hand away. "They are real. I borrowed my daughter's body."

Nina snatched her hand back and held it to her chest, her eyes wide again, locked back on his. "You possessed her?"

"In a manner of speaking." He shrugged. "She is not happy with me. Hell only knows what she is doing to my body right now. I may return to find myself a eunuch."

"I hope not," Nina murmured, strengthening his hope that he stood a chance with her, and then seemed to realise what she had said and set her pretty face in a black scowl and glared at him. "It would serve you right. Do you often body-swap with your daughter?"

She froze.

"You have a daughter?"

Lucifer smiled.

"I do, but it is a long story and not for now, and no, I have never swapped with her before… but you left…" His smile faded and he frowned down into her eyes, losing himself in the sea of pale green perfection that he had thought he would never see again, not like this anyway, with her so close to him and looking at him as if she wanted to be with him, despite everything she knew. "You left and I cannot leave Hell. This was the only way I could reach you."

"Why?" she whispered and edged closer to him, her eyes searching his.

"Because the gates seal me in Hell and I cannot leave unless I—"

She pressed the tip of her finger to his lips, silencing him. "No… why did you want to reach me?"

Lucifer caught her hand, drew it away from his mouth, and pulled down a deep breath, filling his lungs with air that tasted too clean before expelling it slowly in an effort to calm himself as he tried to find the right words.

The ones that would make her come back with him.

The ones that would win her heart.

"I want you to return," he murmured softly and furrowed his eyebrows as he looked into her eyes, hoping she would see in his that he meant every word he was saying, even though he looked like his damned daughter. He had hoped he would be back in his own body when he confessed all of this. "I do not want to be in that place without you, Nina, because without you it is Hell. I believed my daughter had turned me into a sentimental fool, but now I know differently. You came along and showed me just how deeply I could care about someone… just how strongly I could love someone."

A blush crept onto her cheeks and her smile wobbled on her lips.

"Perhaps it was all of you. You… Erin… and Dante."

Her smile faded. "Who's Dante? Your son?"

He shook his head. "My grandson, and another long story, one I will happily share with you when we are safe back in the fortress. Angels will be coming to fight me, Nina. I cannot remain here. I must return, but I will not go without you."

"Back in the castle." Her tone turned distant and he feared he was losing her again, until she lifted her eyes back to his and smiled. "Is it weird that I miss that place?"

Lucifer thought about that. She had called it a prison, and he had once felt that way about it too, but now he knew it to be his home. Was it possible Nina was coming to see his fortress as her home too?

Her nose wrinkled as she looked at him. "It's not as weird as looking at you when you're in a woman's body."

"I hope it is not ruining your attraction to me, because it is a one time event. I find it strange and irritating. Weak." He frowned down at his body. "Everything feels wrong. Besides, I think Erin will, as she crassly puts it, tear me a new one when I return as promised."

Nina grinned. "If she hasn't already torn your body a new one."

Lucifer paled. "Perhaps I should have thought this through more, but I was not thinking. I needed to reach you and make you see that whatever Mihail told you, it was a lie. He brought you to me, and he took you away from me, but he did not make me fall for you."

Her smile softened and he drank the affection that filled her eyes as she looked at him.

He held his hand out to her but she still didn't take it.

He sighed and looked down at his feet, feeling a tug in his breast that he hadn't experienced in a very long time. He was being pulled back to Hell, but it wasn't Heaven's doing. It was Erin. He could almost feel her fury and rage, and could definitely sense the violence she was unleashing in his domain.

"I do not think I will be allowed to see Dante anymore after this."

He didn't realise he had said that aloud until Nina's hand slipped into his and she squeezed it, her voice soft and soothing.

"I'll go with you, but only because I want some answers and I don't think I'll get them if you're busy fighting angels… and I don't want you to have to fight them… I don't want them near me… and I don't want your daughter to be mad at you." The serious edge to her eyes when he met them told him that he hadn't won her yet.

His battle for his little mortal female was only just beginning. He glanced down at her cream sweater, at the flat plane of her stomach. He wanted to press his hand to it and use his power to sense whether she bore his child, even though Mihail's taking her was the only confirmation he really needed.

She didn't want him to fight the angels, but it was inevitable. Heaven would want her in their hands, and that meant he would have to fight for her.

Nina spoke again, the steady tone of her voice drawing his focus back to her and comforting him. "Maybe if she sees that you wanted to leave Hell because of me, she won't be mad?"

That touched him.

He shifted his hand in hers, linking their fingers, and focused on his domain and his fortress that towered in the centre of it. The colourful world around him twisted into darkness and then disappeared, revealing the courtyard of his home.

A huge black blast of energy careened towards him.

Lucifer tugged Nina behind him and threw his free hand forwards, deflecting the orb before it could strike him and Nina. It shot off to his right and crashed into the spires of rock there, causing them to explode.

Lucifer growled and straightened his spine, trying to ignore how strange it was to face himself in a battle. "Behave yourself, Daughter, because you almost hit our guest."

His body's left eyebrow quirked. Lucifer kept pace with it as it moved side to side, his daughter attempting to peer past him.

Erin huffed and folded her arms across her chest. Behind her, the walls of his fortress began to repair themselves, the huge cracks in the black stone sealing shut. His daughter had been busy while he had been gone. Many of the spires that surrounded the courtyard were ruined too, laying in rubble, their broken remains spewing lava as they attempted to rebuild themselves.

"I want my body back." It was odd hearing himself say those words. Whenever he thought he had a grasp on things, that he was used to seeing his body and hearing his voice and could comprehend that it was Erin inside it, and Erin talking, it all felt weird again. She planted her hands on her hips. His hips. Weird. "Unless you intend to feed Dante come my little hellion's dinner time?"

Lucifer looked down at his breasts and pulled a face. "I think not. You can have your body back. I have what I wanted."

He focused on his hand and on his body, and black lightning leaped the gap between his palm and his body's forehead. Pain exploded inside his skull and he flinched away, pressed his hands to his head and growled as he tried to tamp it down. It slowly faded and he opened his eyes, exhaling a sigh of relief when he saw his own flat broad chest and a suit rather than breasts and a summer dress.

Lucifer turned to face Nina, and saw only the castle.

Fuck.

He spun on the spot, coming to face Erin where she stood right next to Nina. He hadn't thought about the fact he would leave Nina near his daughter when switching back into his own body. Fear lanced him, turning his blood to ice in his veins, and he lifted his hand to reach for Nina, convinced that his daughter would steal her away from him, teleporting her beyond his reach once more.

Erin just looked her up and down. "Did he kidnap you too?"

Nina flicked him a curious glance and then looked back at Erin and shook her head. "No. I think an angel did."

"Mihail. He's such a bastard." Erin snorted and then shrugged. "Pops kidnapped me once. I figured he kidnapped everyone he liked."

Lucifer arched an eyebrow at that. Nina looked at him in a way that left him feeling she was trying to put the name "pops" together with what she knew about him and was failing to make them fit.

Erin pointed at him, a corona of red surrounding her golden irises. "You're banned from seeing Dante for a month, and if you try that shit again, I'm telling Veiron. It freaked me the fuck out."

Lucifer nodded in agreement with that. "It was not pleasant."

He held his hand out to Nina.

"Lucifer…" She started and Erin's eyes almost popped out of her head, her lips twitching into a wicked smile that made him growl and glare at her in warning.

"I have something extra juicy to tell Veiron and the Scooby gang," Erin singsonged and Lucifer advanced on her.

She didn't relent. Her smile only grew wider, more wicked.

"Oh, they're going to love finding out your real name."

Lucifer gave up attempting to threaten her. It wasn't any fun when the person you were threatening wasn't afraid of you and knew they could match your power blow for blow and come out of a fight with you unscathed.

He looked at his daughter, seeing for the first time just how strong she truly was. She had held her own against angels and demons, had taken on the world more than once, and always came to the aid of her friends and family, but her true strength rested in a part of her he had never wanted to acknowledge before.

Her heart.

She loved deeply, unconditionally, and as he looked at her as she spoke to Nina with a smile on her lips and laughter in her eyes, he had the feeling that it wasn't something she had somehow inherited from her mother, because her genes were a perfect match for his.

He had bottled his memories of the time that had come before his tenure in Hell, had closed himself off to the male he had once been, but he could no longer shut out the past.

Because the very image of the man he had once been stood before him.

His daughter.

He had laughed like her once, had cherished those he had considered family and friends, and would have done anything to protect the ones that he loved with all of his heart.

His gaze slid to Nina and she stopped giggling, her expression turning serious as she slowly brought her gaze to meet his.

Perhaps that male wasn't dead and gone.

Perhaps he had only been buried and the catalyst of his resurrection was looking at him with love in her eyes.

Erin made a gagging noise.

Lucifer sighed and scowled at her, but it lasted only a second before his temper faded and concern filled his heart. She was strong, but that didn't make her invincible, and he wasn't sure he could cope if he lost her or his grandson. Her features shifted, her grin fading and expression becoming uncomfortable.

"Do not trust the angels of the apocalypse, Daughter." Lucifer took measured steps towards her and placed his right hand on her shoulder as he looked down into her eyes. "Mihail delivered Nina to me and Mihail took her back to the mortal world. The male has issues with me, and I would not put it past him to take those issues out on you now that Nina is back within my realm. Be careful."

Erin huffed and glared at him. "Spoilsport. Now I don't feel like taking the piss out of you over your name. I'll be careful. Always am."

He didn't like the flippant way she said that. She was dealing with more than mere angels and demons now. Mihail and his cohorts were dangerous, and so were their originals, the princes of Hell.

"Promise me, Daughter. Take every precaution and do not lower your guard." He gently squeezed her shoulder and her look turned even more uncomfortable.

She shrugged out of his grasp, fidgeted with the hem of her dress, and then nodded and turned away from him, walking towards the plateau.

She raised her hand and waved without looking back at him. "Now I know where I got it from."

Lucifer frowned at her retreating back. "Got what from?"

She tossed a grin over her shoulder, her amber eyes bright and sparkling with it. "The sentimental fool gene."

She disappeared.

Lucifer huffed. "Sometimes, Daughter, you deserve punishment for your impudence."

The feel of Nina's eyes on him, burning into him, drew his focus across to her where she stood just feet from him. She was grinning too.

He scowled. "What?"

She only smiled wider. "I know you won't punish her. You clearly love your daughter."

As uncomfortable as hearing that made him, there was a part of him that could no longer deny it. He sighed again and looked off into the distance at the dark lands of his realm, his senses locked on Erin where she had just appeared on her island.

"Do not tell anyone," he said without looking at Nina.

The back of her hand brushed his and he looked down at her. She shrugged. "Who do you think I'm going to tell about any of this? Everyone would think I'd gone crazy. I still sort of think I've gone crazy."

He reached up and swept his fingers across her cheek, clearing the rogue wavy strands of her auburn hair back behind her ear.

"You have not gone crazy, Nina." He feathered his fingers down her cheek again, along the line of her jaw to her chin, and pressed his thumb there, keeping her looking up into his eyes. "But you have driven me crazy."

She hesitated, a war erupting in her eyes, one that made him want to take back his words because he was pushing her too hard again. He had promised to give her answers if she came with him, and he meant to do just that. He had to confess everything and then it would be down to her to make a decision that he knew would be difficult for her.

"I have realised why Mihail chose you, Nina, and what his plan was for you."

Her cheeks paled, her green eyes growing enormous as her fear trickled into him through the point where they touched.

"What?" she whispered, her voice shaking so much that he ached to comfort her, even when he knew that what he was about to tell her would only scare her further.

But he needed to be honest with her, because he wasn't sure what he was going to do if he was right.

He feared the first woman to steal his heart would end up stolen from him and he would be left with nothing but a solemn yet beautiful reminder of what he had lost.

He lowered his free hand to her stomach, denied the urge to use his powers to seek an answer to the question burning in his heart, aware that it might hurt Nina and any child she carried, and held her gaze.

"They wanted you to have my child."

CHAPTER 14

Nina stared up into Lucifer's golden eyes, sure that she had heard him wrong. Her hand fell to her stomach and she tensed when it touched his where it rested over her belly button. It wasn't possible. Maybe Heaven didn't know that.

She shook her head at such a ridiculous thought, sure that whatever higher powers existed in this world, they knew what they were doing and they had chosen her for a reason.

Lucifer frowned at her, his head tilting to his right, and searched her eyes. "You do not believe me?"

"I'm not sure what I believe anymore, Lucifer." She stepped back, needing the space and some air. Her stomach turned when she sucked down a sharp breath, getting a hit of thick, moist and rank air rather than the clear crispness that she needed. Her throat tightened and a weight settled on her chest, pressing down on it harder the longer she stared into Lucifer's eyes.

The more she saw the belief in them.

Mihail had called him a liar, but the only one she knew had lied to her was the angel himself. Lucifer hadn't been honest with her, but when she kept her head and tried to look at it from his perspective, she could understand why. He had known that she would freak out and run away from him, rushing headlong into what she felt sure was a very dangerous realm and into the arms of an even more dangerous man.

That man was an angel, with the white wings to prove it in every clichéd way possible, but she hadn't felt safe with him. Her heart had warned her not to trust him and her instincts had told her that he was dangerous, out to get something from her and poison her against Lucifer for some reason.

Was it really possible that that reason was the fact that she was pregnant?

"I can't believe it," she muttered and kept shaking her head, struggling to believe that there might be life inside her already. "Why would they choose me? I don't understand why they would choose me. It doesn't make any sense. It just doesn't... and you already have a daughter. Why would they want you to make another one?"

He moved a step nearer to her and she resisted the urge to back off another one, torn between allowing him to close the gap between them so she could draw comfort from his proximity and pushing him away so she could have the space she desperately needed.

The air grew thicker and she wheezed as she tried to pull it down into her lungs.

Lucifer's expression darkened, he caught hold of her arm before she could move, and suddenly it was dark and she couldn't see anything. She tried to wrestle free of him but his grip tightened and he tugged her against his hard body, his arms wrapping around her to pin her to his chest. When the darkness receded, she found herself standing in the apartment he had given her during her stay.

She hadn't really had time to process the fact that he could apparently teleport when he had taken her from London. She wasn't sure she'd had enough time to process anything that had happened since she had awoken on his chaise longue in that gothic room to find him watching her. It had all been a whirlwind of craziness that still challenged her to a degree, muddling her emotions and leaving her unsure of what she was doing and whether she had actually lost her mind.

His fingers brushed her cheek, the caress so light that it wreaked havoc on her strength, tearing it away from her until she wanted nothing more than to lean into his touch and allow him to be strong for her.

She couldn't do that.

She had done that before and it had only ended with her hurt and alone.

She pushed his hand away and paced across the room, breathing deep of the fresher air and using the time to clear her head so she could at least think straight and ask the right questions. Lucifer's gaze tracked her, heating her as it increased in intensity, threatening to wreck her focus. She tossed him a glare, one she hoped warned him to give her some space and time.

"I will explain everything. I do not expect it will do me any favours, but I have made a promise to be honest with you, and that is what I will be." He leaned his bottom against the back of the couch, pressed his palms against the black wooden frame and curled his fingers over the red velvet.

A single glance at him was enough to tell her that he expected whatever confession he was about to make to do far worse than paint him in a slightly bad light.

He expected her to despise him, and it was clearly hurting him.

And that messed with her head worse than anything up to this point.

He was the Devil. The original fallen angel. Ruler of Hell. A very bad person if the stories were anything to go by. If bad person was a way of saying the most evil being in the world.

But as she looked at him where he leaned opposite her, a look in his golden eyes that spoke of fear and resignation, laced with a touch of defeat and a dash of hope, she couldn't see a monster.

He had been cold and distant at times, but he had been warm more times than that. He had been kind and considerate, affectionate even. She had seen a man who clearly loved his daughter and who was pained by the thought he wouldn't be allowed to see his grandson. She had been with a man who had been gentle with her, had sought to please her and had protected her. Everything she knew about him went against the picture of the Devil she had grown up with.

But she wasn't about to let that fool her into believing that all of it had been real.

She was determined to keep her head, view things objectively, listen to everything he had to say and think everything over before she made any move of her own.

Lucifer glanced down at his polished leather shoes, his handsome face settling in sombre lines that made her want to go to him, sweep her fingers across his sculpted cheek and make him look at her. She wanted to ease his pain, and it took all of her willpower to remain where she was and deny that need.

"You know who I am… and I am sure you can guess what that means. I am by no means a good man, Nina. I was shaped by circumstance into what I am today. I was used, my loyalty betrayed, and I was weak when I should have been strong." He frowned at his shoes, the black slashes of his eyebrows dipping together above eyes slowly turning red. Fangs flashed between his lips as he spoke, and as she stood there watching the changes happening, she realised that she no longer feared him when he looked like this. He flicked a glance at her and she schooled her features, hiding her feelings from him. She built a wall around them, shielding them from his steady gaze, unwilling to reveal them to him when she was still uncertain of everything because she feared he would use them against her somehow.

She had been manipulated too many times to count and she had made a promise that it would never happen again.

Her mind supplied that it was too late and that promise was already broken. The angel had manipulated her and, for all she knew, Lucifer had too.

Her heart rebelled against that. Lucifer had said that she had seduced him, and deep in her heart she knew that it hadn't been a lie to convince her to come with him or make her believe him.

"Go on," she whispered when he didn't look as if he had the heart to continue.

"I swore vengeance against those who had betrayed me, Nina. I turned my prison into my palace and I reigned with an iron fist." He lowered his eyes to the floor at her feet. She could believe that he had plotted revenge, because hadn't she done the same when she had been hurt? She had tried to lash out at her ex-husband by showing him how wonderful her life was without him when his had gone to hell. She had wanted to hurt him. Lucifer had wanted to do the same, only his plan for revenge was far bigger than hers and she had the feeling the consequences of it would be far greater. "As part of my plan, I have spent millennia attempting to... sire offspring."

Nina didn't need to see his eyes to know what he meant by that. "You seduced women... angels?"

He shook his head. "There are no female angels. I... only mortal females can carry my offspring."

Cold slithered through her veins and she curled her fingers into fists as a viper hissed in her heart, whispering words that stoked her anger and made her want to back another step away from him, because she felt he was going to hurt her. The urge to lash out and deal the first blow was too strong, overwhelming her as it had always done since she had left her ex-husband, keeping her closed off from the world and protected inside her bubble.

A bubble that had begun to feel lonely, but still felt like a necessity to her.

It saved her from being hurt by others.

And Lucifer was going to destroy her when he realised that Heaven had brought him the wrong woman to knock up.

"So you're saying you've been sleeping with every woman available in order to make yourself a child... bringing them to this place... probably to this room right?"

"No, Nina." He pushed off, rising onto his feet, and shook his head. She shook hers right back at him and held her hand out, silently warning him to keep his distance. Devil or not, if he came near her, she wouldn't be able to stop herself from slapping him right now. "I never brought them here."

"Well, that's comforting."

His jaw muscle twitched. "I know it does not sound good. I am confessing that I have slept with many women, but I have not been with a woman in months."

"Months?" She barked out a laugh. "Wow… way to hold yourself back. So because you've been keeping it in your pants for a few months, Heaven just decided to stick me in your path… knowing you'd be horny… and that makes me what… just another inevitable notch on your bedpost?"

Her heart hurt and she pulled down a deep breath, resisted the temptation to rub her chest, and refused to let the tears stinging the backs of her eyes make an appearance. She should have stayed in her apartment in London. She shouldn't have let Lucifer sweep her up in everything again, making her foolishly believe that somehow everything would miraculously end up perfect for her.

There was nothing perfect about this situation.

She had fallen in love with the Devil.

It didn't get more messed up than that.

She folded her arms across her chest and began pacing again, needing the automatic motion to give her something to focus on so she could clear her head.

"Nina," Lucifer whispered but she refused to look at him, fearing that if she did, she would lose her fragile grip on her heart and it would betray her and leap the gap to him. "There is something different about you. You are the first female I did not want to sleep with."

Nina turned on him with a glare, her blood catching fire on hearing that. "Well, that's lovely. How noble of you to sleep with me when you didn't want to."

He flinched away from her and then rallied, reaching his left hand out to her. She scowled at it, turned her nose up and resumed pacing. Faster now. Her swift agitated strides carried her back and forth across the expansive room, her trainers squeaking occasionally on the obsidian stone floor.

Lucifer raked his fingers through his black hair, messing it up as he tugged at the lengths and gritted his teeth. Frustration flashed in his eyes as she glanced at him, but other emotions shone in them too, ones she had never seen before and gave her pause.

Where was the confident man he had been around her for most of the time they had been together?

He had shown her a vulnerable side of himself, but there had always been a sliver of confidence remaining in his gaze, as if he was sure of himself despite allowing her to see his weakness.

His weary sigh kept her gaze on him and her pacing slowed, concern beginning to outweigh the other emotions in her heart.

"It was not an act of nobility, Nina. You were the first woman I did not want to sleep with because I feared…" He gritted his teeth again, growled through them, and clawed at his hair. "Fuck… I fear… so much that you are in on this plan and that you will leave me… and that… that would… I have survived atrocities… torture so vile… but nothing I have suffered… none of it broke me… but if you left me… that would destroy me."

Her vision blurred as hot tears filled her eyes, causing Lucifer to wobble out of focus. She scrubbed them away and looked at him with clear eyes and an even clearer heart. His heart was in his eyes for her to see, every emotion that had been in his words as he had laid that fragile part of himself on the line, and no matter what she told herself, she couldn't bring herself to believe what Mihail had told her.

He wasn't a liar.

No one could pretend to look so broken and distraught, filled with pain at the mere thought that she felt nothing for him and that everything they had shared had been an act on her part.

She believed him when he said that her leaving would wound him, because her soul screamed that it would wound her too.

Her eyes searched his, and the longer she looked into them, the clearer his feelings became to her.

She already had wounded him.

She had hurt him by leaving with the angel and he had risked everything important to him in order to bring her back to him, and to keep her safe as he had promised.

He had risked alienating himself from the daughter and grandchild that he clearly loved.

The gravity of that hit her hard, knocking her a step towards him. It hit her in a good way, because for the first time in what felt like forever, she knew what it felt like to be loved and wanted.

She had found a man willing to stand at her side, one who would break all the rules and move mountains to be with her, and he hadn't asked anything of her.

He only wanted her to give him a chance.

Lucifer looked away from her, towards the tapestry to his right that covered the door to the valley, and closed his eyes.

"I was rash... I should have thought things through... and I cannot apologise enough for the danger I have placed you in, Nina." He sighed and his chin dipped towards his chest, and she silently cursed him for making her want to cross the small stretch of black stone flags to him and wrap her arms around him to comfort him.

It seemed insane that the Devil needed comfort, but everything about him said that he needed it more than anything right now. She was close to surrendering to the pressing need to give him something to soothe him, a sliver of hope at the very least, when he opened his eyes and frowned at the floor, his words freezing her to the spot and chilling her heart.

"Part of me hopes that what we have done does not result in a pregnancy."

Nina's hands came to rest on her stomach, her fingers curling to clutch the soft cream cashmere sweater. "Why?"

Her voice trembled and she knew he had heard her fear when he lifted his head and looked at her. She couldn't find her voice, could scarcely breathe as emotions flooded her. She struggled with her feelings, trying to get hold of herself and quieten the part of herself that desperately wanted a child, afraid that thinking about the possibility she might be pregnant would only lead to her being hurt. She told herself on repeat that it wasn't possible, and as soon as Lucifer realised that, he would no longer want to be with her.

He wouldn't stand by her after all.

His steady gaze questioned her back and she couldn't stop the words from spilling from her lips as her feelings rose up against her, owning her and stealing control, too powerful for her to contain.

"I know you have children, and I understand that sometimes men will settle for having children from another woman in their life—"

"Who did such a thing to you?" Lucifer interjected, his expression rapidly darkening.

She turned her cheek to him and bit her tongue to silence herself as thoughts of her ex-husband flooded her mind, making her heart ache. Tears lined her lashes again and she screwed her eyes shut, pulled down a sharp breath, and exhaled it hard.

Warm fingers brushing her cheek made her jerk her head up, her eyes flicking open to lock with Lucifer's where he towered over her. The concern in his golden gaze stole her breath away and she stared into his eyes as she absorbed the comfort of his caress, stealing every last drop of it to restore her strength and put her feet back on solid ground.

If the tales were right, he would know if she lied.

They were beyond hiding things from each other anyway.

He had been honest with her, and now it was her turn to be honest with him.

"I was married… but he left me when…" Heck, it was harder than she had thought it would be. Her throat tightened and she struggled to gather enough courage to tell Lucifer about her past and share a piece of herself that she had never shared with anyone. She pushed the words out. "I was told by close to a dozen doctors, from regular ones to the most expensive physicians my ex-husband could buy, that I can never have children."

Lucifer's handsome face darkened again.

Her hands tightened against her stomach. "He left me for another woman and had the family he wanted with her instead."

"He cast you out… he betrayed your loyalty and love for him." He practically snarled those words, his deep voice a thick growl as his eyes narrowed and a corona of fire blazed around his irises.

Nina suddenly understood why she felt so connected to Lucifer, had always had the sense that they were kindred spirits. Her husband had betrayed her, just as Lucifer had said. He had taken her love for him, and he had broken her heart. She searched Lucifer's eyes as the gold slowly bled into crimson, seeing in them familiar pain.

Suffering born of betrayal.

"I moved on with my life." She flexed her fingers against her sweater, barely resisting the need to touch Lucifer's cheek and comfort him.

Her words seemed to draw him back from whatever dark place he had gone to and he blinked, his irises clearing as he looked down into her eyes.

She had moved on with her life, but she could see that Lucifer hadn't moved on with his.

He had chosen the other path, the one that had looked dark to her but had inevitably drawn her to it when her ex-husband had contacted her about meeting up.

He had chosen revenge.

And now she had been pulled into a plot against him and she still didn't understand why she had been chosen.

"So you see, Heaven picked the wrong woman," she said with a smile that she didn't feel in her heart, because that part of her wanted to be the right woman for the man standing in front of her.

She wanted to be what he needed her to be—his strength, his courage to rise onto his feet and choose the right path. She wanted to give him a reason to set aside whatever plan he had to avenge himself.

But she wasn't sure she had the power to do it.

She had seen him with his daughter. No matter what he had said, family was important to him, and that was the one thing she couldn't give to him.

"It isn't possible that I'm pregnant, Lucifer. Not unless the doctors were wrong." She went to back away, but he caught her hand, pulled her up against him and wrapped one arm around her waist to lock her against his chest.

He smoothed his free hand over her hair.

"They were not wrong… and if it were anyone else you had slept with…" He growled low in his throat, his eyes flashing crimson and his fangs on show as his lips peeled back off them. That brief flare of anger heated her blood, made her heart beat a little quicker as it whispered that he was jealous. "It would not have resulted in a pregnancy. I have a very special ability. I can make a barren womb fertile and receptive to me."

Nina's eyes slowly widened and a shiver danced down her spine and arms.

Her mind went blank and she could only stare up into his eyes as she took that in and processed it.

"But you don't want me to be pregnant." Those words left her lips of their own volition, rising up from her heart.

"It is not because I do not desire children, Nina. It is because of the risk to you. I have finally found something that I want to keep hold of and not lose, and I fear…" He chuckled mirthlessly. "I have not missed that emotion, but you certainly bring it out in me. I fear that I will lose you because the baby will be too powerful. I will lose you both."

She didn't need to ask to know that was the reason he only had one daughter even when he had been trying to father children for a long time. She pressed her hands to her stomach, a trickle of fear running through her, clashing with the hope in her heart.

Erin had survived though, and that gave her hope a boost.

With that boost, she found strength that had been dormant in her, determination that she embraced as she stood a little straighter and held Lucifer's gaze.

"I've been through too much pain and loneliness to let something like this kill me. If I am pregnant, I won't let anything stop me from bringing this child into the world, because it's everything I've ever wanted, and you gave it to me… and that only makes it more beautiful."

Lucifer averted his gaze, looking beyond her right shoulder. "No female who has borne my offspring has ever survived."

Cold stole through her, but she refused to let it take hold and stir her fear again. "What about Erin?"

"Her mother died at birth." The solemn edge his eyes gained had her raising her hand and placing it gently against his cheek.

She drew him back to face her, so his eyes locked with hers, and managed to smile, hoping it would alleviate his fear together with what she was about to say.

"I've seen how powerful you are, but you don't seem to be all powerful."

He frowned at that, and she knew he felt she was belittling him, but it didn't stop her.

"I guess Erin's mother gave birth naturally?"

He shrugged. "I cannot honestly say I was keeping track."

It was her turn to frown at him. She didn't want to ask how many women he had slept with over the years, but it was obviously enough that he'd developed a habit of seducing them and then sending them back to their world, and had probably used whatever powers he had to tell if a child had been born from their union.

His expression shifted, gaining a nervous edge that almost made her smile, because it told her something and it was the only thing she needed to know.

That part of his life was behind him now.

Somehow, she had captured this magnificent, if not a little dangerous and dark, man before her and now he only had eyes for her.

Eyes that were filled with affection and hope, together with fear that she wanted to remove for him.

"I'll ignore that comment," she said and relief joined the emotions in his gaze. "Do you think that it's childbirth that kills the mother and not the baby?"

It was a frightening prospect that if she was pregnant, the baby growing inside her might actually attempt to kill her. She pushed that thought aside, trying to focus on finding a solution to the problem, because she was damned if she was going to die now that she had a reason to live.

Lucifer's gaze turned thoughtful. "I believe it is the strain of the birth on the mother. When the baby attempts to draw all the power it can from her in order to survive, it kills her."

Just how powerful would his baby be? As powerful as he was?

A flash of Erin hurling great orbs of black energy against the walls of the fortress blasted into her mind and she had to fight to supress the shudder that wracked her. Erin had seemed as powerful as Lucifer. If she had been that way since before birth, it was little wonder the mother hadn't survived.

But Nina might.

No, she would.

She smiled at Lucifer, who responded by giving her a quizzical look that asked if she had gone mad.

She had gone mad the moment she had met him, just as he had gone crazy when he had met her. This whole scenario was insane, but her heart said to run with it, because she felt at home here in Lucifer's arms, looking up into his eyes. That heart beat faster when he brushed his fingers across her cheek and murmured soft words to her in a language she didn't understand, the sound of his deep voice curling around her making her melt into him and distracting her.

She leaned into his lips as he pressed them to her cheek and then pulled herself back together and pushed her hands against his chest, breaking free of him so they could finish their conversation.

They were a long way from done.

"I might have the answer."

Those five words seem to hit their mark because he stopped attempting to get closer to her and frowned down at her, a sceptical edge to his handsome face.

"You do?"

Nina nodded. "Caesarean."

Lucifer's left eyebrow shot up and she had to stifle a giggle. Her all powerful Lucifer evidently lacked knowledge about certain matters.

"Many women these days have to give birth through a C-section. They cut the baby out of them when it reaches term in order to avoid complications."

His eyes widened. "They cut it out of you?"

The horrified edge to his expression and tone had her raising her eyebrows at him for a change. It seemed so strange to her, almost comical and wrong. By his own confession, he had suffered through torture that had no doubt left those marks on his back, and as much as she didn't want to think about it, he had probably dealt out a lot worse to others. Yet, the thought of professional trained surgeons operating to remove a baby from its mother apparently disturbed him and seemed barbaric judging by his reaction.

"It's perfectly safe," Nina said. "My own mother gave birth to me that way. If I am pregnant, it would avoid the problem of the birth triggering the baby's natural instinct to suck the life from me."

It seemed so wrong that the part of that sentence that freaked her out was the start of it where she had mentioned the possibility of there being life growing inside of her, but she didn't care. She was rolling with this crazy train, because the destination was the man holding her in his arms so gently that it was as if he feared he might break her and looking at her with a wealth of love in his eyes. He had changed her life, and she knew she had changed his too, and both had been for the better.

"It might not stop it from happening." He feathered his fingertips across her cheek and fear surfaced in his golden eyes again. "I would have to find other methods... ways of keeping you safe."

It touched her that he desired that, very deeply by the looks of him, and she nodded.

"You will stay then?" he whispered.

Nina looked up into his eyes, watching the way his emotions played out in them, realising that they were never cold when he was looking at her, not anymore. The fear in them steadily increased as she thought about what he was asking, thought about everything she would be leaving behind and thought about who he was.

The Devil.

A fallen angel.

The fallen angel.

Whenever she thought about that, there was a part of her that said she was crazy to be considering staying with him. In Hell. Where he no doubt spent his days terrorising souls just as the stories said he did. Those souls might deserve the torment they suffered, but that didn't mean she could condone it or be comfortable with it.

She had felt there was darkness in him, but she hadn't expected that darkness to be as strong as it was. She had expected it to be more like the sliver of darkness in her heart, the sort that many people carried with them.

But now she realised that while she held only a sliver of darkness inside her, he held only a sliver of light.

He was darkness.

He was the being that most mortals feared.

She studied his eyes, trying to see that being, but only saw Lucifer looking back at her. She only saw the man who had been kind to her, had fought to protect her, and had risked everything he held dear to bring her back to him.

But would she always see him that way?

Would she continue to feel love for him when she finally saw the darker part of himself that she knew he was hiding from her?

She dropped her gaze to his chest, closed her eyes as her mind churned, and then lifted her head and looked up at him as the answer came to her.

"Lucifer—"

The entire castle shook and Lucifer's arms tightened around her, keeping her upright as the floor trembled so violently her knees gave out. Her heart pounded, her fingers grasping the chest of his suit jacket as she squeezed her eyes shut and pressed against him. He covered her head with his hands, shielding her as dust rained down.

The quake stopped as quickly as it had started.

Lucifer eased back and she emerged from his arms, and looked up at him.

Black wings made of shadows covered her. Polished obsidian horns curled from behind Lucifer's now-pointed ears, parting his jet hair as they flared forwards beside his temples into fierce points. Blazing red eyes held hers. His lips peeled back off his fangs as he snarled, the sound startling her almost as much as his appearance, but not as much as the word he growled.

That single word struck fear into her heart.

"Mihail."

CHAPTER 15

Lucifer teleported directly to the courtyard of his fortress, leaving Nina in the safety of her room and landing just metres from his enemy.

Enemies.

He snarled at Mihail and the six guardian angels flanking him, their polished silver-edged blue armour bright against the black backdrop of the spires of rock that enclosed the courtyard. Each male stood with their silver-blue wings furled against their backs and each wielded a curved silver blade, held point down at their side, close to the strips of armour that shielded their hips. None were a match for Lucifer. He could kill every one of them with a thought.

Or turn them to his side with little more than a push using his voice.

They were weak.

Their leader was not and Lucifer knew from experience that the angel wouldn't give him a chance to exert the power of his voice on the angels at his back.

Mihail stood a few feet in front of them, his white wings drifting down to rest against his back. The dull black armour he wore shifted as he moved a step, the chest plate rising as he inhaled.

He wielded no weapon.

"Return the female to us."

Lucifer chuckled at that and grinned at the angel.

"She will remain with me." He canted his head and flexed his fingers at his sides, biding his time as he studied his opponent.

He wouldn't allow Mihail near Nina, and he wouldn't make the same mistake as he had the last time they had fought. He wouldn't let Mihail trick him into firing on his own fortress. As long as Nina remained inside it, she would be safe.

Wingbeats filled the air, the steady drone making his grin stretch wider.

Mihail lifted icy eyes to the air above Lucifer and glared at the Hell's angels descending behind him. The six men touched down, their black leather boots silent as they made contact with the obsidian stone floor. Lucifer issued them a mental command, ordering them to shield the castle from their intruders while he dealt with them.

Unlike Mihail, he hadn't brought weaker angels to do his dirty work. He intended to take Mihail down by himself, without anyone interfering.

This was his fight.

"Hand the mortal female over." Mihail drew a white blade from the air and pointed it at Lucifer.

He responded by shaking his head.

Snarled.

"Never."

Mihail kicked off, but Lucifer was already moving, his shadow wings beating the thick air as he shot towards the angel. He threw his left hand forwards, sending ribbons of darkness rocketing towards Mihail. They broke apart when they reached him, rendering the urgent swipe of his sword redundant, and shot around him. Mihail's blue eyes widened and he looked off to his left.

Lucifer sneered at the three guardian angels there.

Mihail's white wings hammered the air and his body twisted, his left boot touching the ground. He kicked off, propelling himself towards the guardian angels. He wouldn't be fast enough.

Lucifer's shadows divided again and he turned away from them, leaving them to do their work while he shifted his focus to the remaining three angels.

Mihail should have brought more allies with him.

An agonised bellow filled the air as the first of his shadows struck, slithering around the neck of one of the guardian angels. The male went down in a heap as it tightened, strangling him. The other two angels fought valiantly, their silver swords bright blurs against the darkness. Mihail joined them and Lucifer growled as the angel raised his hand and white light shot down from the vault of Hell, engulfing the three guardian angels.

Dissipating Lucifer's shadows.

It seemed Mihail had gained control over some new powers since their battle millennia ago.

Ones that Lucifer didn't like.

"You dare call on the light in my realm?" Lucifer kicked off and ran at Mihail.

The angel turned swiftly to face him, his white ponytail sweeping in an arc behind him and his blade cutting through the air. Lucifer teleported, easily evading the blow, and appeared above him. He roared as he tossed his hand forwards at the same time as he beat his wings to carry him higher, clear of the blast zone of the black ball of energy he hurled at Mihail.

Mihail beat his wings and flew hard, tossing a grim look over his shoulder at the same time.

He launched forwards as the orb struck the ground where he had been and grunted as the blast struck his back, sending him tumbling head over heels through the air. His roar of pain was music to Lucifer's ears as he hit the wall of the courtyard and slid down it to land in a heap, his white wings covered in black dust.

The three angels he had protected didn't fare so well.

The blast caught the right foot of the fastest, devouring it and sending the angel crashing onto his face.

It cut through the lower half of the second and a beam of golden light shot down, reclaiming the fallen male and returning him to Heaven.

It hit the third male head on.

No light claimed him.

Mihail lifted his head, his eyes wide and filled with horror as he looked across the courtyard to the remains of the male.

"No." He raised his eyes to Lucifer and the disbelief in them tugged at his heart.

"Someone neglected to mention to you that you are not the only one with new powers." Lucifer drifted down to land on the flagstones of the courtyard. "He will wander Hell as nothing more than a spirit now, tormented in the shadows… for eternity. Withdraw your men before they suffer the same fate. Leave my realm."

Mihail shoved onto his hands and knees, steely resolve filling his pale blue eyes as he set his jaw. He rose onto his feet, dusted himself off, and called his blade back to him.

"I will not leave without her." The angel swept the sword down at his side. "I did not ask for this mission, but I will not fail in it. I will carry out my duty, or I will die trying."

Those words struck a chord in Lucifer, one that only stirred the darkness inside him. Mihail didn't agree with his orders. He was doing this out of loyalty to his master. Lucifer had been in his position, knew how the male felt, how it must torment him to do something he didn't agree with, but he couldn't give the angel what he wanted.

He couldn't allow Mihail to carry out his duty.

The male would have to settle for dying while trying.

Lucifer shrugged, causing his black wings to shift with the motion. "Very well."

His fingers twitched at his sides, his shadows flowing from them, eager to tear into his old adversary and end him this time.

He raised his hand to launch his next attack.

"Wait." Nina's soft voice cutting through the thick silence snapped his focus towards her where she stood in front of the now-open doors of his fortress, out of breath, her cheeks flushed.

Lucifer cursed as he realised the reason the damned doors kept opening for her even though he had adjusted the wards so they wouldn't. It was because she bore his child. The doors recognised his blood in her and that kept overriding the command to remain locked to her.

Mihail slowly smiled.

Victoriously.

"Nina!" Lucifer launched his shadows towards Mihail at the same time as he teleported towards her.

He reappeared in time to see the angel evading the ribbons of darkness and coming straight at him, his wings pinned back as he flew hard.

Lucifer flicked his left hand towards the angel, releasing another blast of energy and then another. The smaller orbs zoomed towards Mihail. The male rolled, set his right foot down on the ground and kicked off, changing direction. The first blast hit the ground where he had been. The second changed course, tracking the angel as he continued on his trajectory.

Aiming straight for Nina.

Never.

Darkness raged through Lucifer, stronger than he had felt it in a long time. Stronger than it had ever been since he had set himself up as ruler of Hell. He felt the changes as they happened to him. The ache in his skull as his horns grew longer. The pain in his fingertips as his nails became long black talons. The cold as his skin paled to white and his lips darkened to black.

The burn as his eyes blazed crimson with the fires of Hell.

"Stay back," he snarled at Nina where she stood behind him, her fear trickling through his veins, increasing his fury and his need to protect her.

She was mortal.

Weak.

Vulnerable.

He needed to protect her, both from Mihail and from himself. It would be too easy for him to kill her by mistake with his power when she was outside the fortress, exposed to the battle.

Why the fuck had she placed herself in danger?

"I don't want to go with you!" She hurled those words at Mihail.

The venom in them surprised Lucifer but it was the meaning in them that shocked him, distracting him for a moment as he took in what she was saying.

She wanted to stay with him.

Pain burst through him, the air blasting from his lungs as something hit him hard, taking him down onto the ground. He skidded across it, a weight pressing down on him, and grunted as fresh agony erupted in his shoulder, the white-hot blaze stealing from him what little breath he had gathered.

Mihail grinned down at him and shoved forwards. Lucifer bellowed at the black vault of Hell as the white blade cut deeper into his right shoulder.

Piercing light erupted within him, driving his shadows back, and he cried out again, tears cutting lines down his temples as he fought the pain, clinging to consciousness.

"Lucifer!" Nina's shriek, filled with fear and agony, roused his strength and he clawed at Mihail, somehow managed to grab the bastard's arm and shove upwards.

The sword pulled free of his flesh and he twisted with the angel, shoving him onto his back and pinning his wings at a painful angle beneath his body. Lucifer growled and punched him across the jaw, snapping his head to his right. Mihail grunted and swung with his blade.

Lucifer rolled to his right, grimaced as he landed on his injured shoulder, and onto his feet.

He threw his hand forwards the moment he hit them, hurling a blast of shadows at Mihail. The angel's blade cut through them as it caught fire, burning with pale flames.

Lucifer launched more shadows at him, forcing him to flee in order to avoid them and buying himself some time. When the angel was at a distance again, regrouped with the remains of his men, Lucifer pressed his left hand to his shoulder and funnelled his power into it.

He screamed as fire ripped through him, staggered backwards and pulled his hand away from his shoulder.

Blood coated his white palm, the red stark against it.

He couldn't heal the wound.

He lifted his head and glared across the gap between him and Mihail. The look in the angel's eyes said that he had known his blade would deal wounds that Lucifer couldn't heal on the fly with his power.

Cursed Heavenly blade.

Lucifer bared his fangs at it.

He was going to get his hands on that blade and destroy it.

Without it, Mihail was nothing but a gnat, ready to be squashed out of existence.

Mihail swept the blade forwards, pointing it towards him.

Lucifer growled as he realised the angel hadn't pointed at him.

The remaining three guardian angels moved as one, their silver-blue wings pounding the air as they took flight, heading straight towards his fortress.

Towards Nina.

Lucifer roared and teleported, appearing in the air before them. Each readied his curved silver blade and flew harder, the ones on either side breaking away from the one on the middle. He sent his shadows after them, his focus on the central angel. The male kept flying at him, his green eyes filled with hatred and determination.

Lucifer had seen that look in a thousand angels' eyes. They had all wanted to be the one to take him down and claim the glory. Fools.

They had all looked differently when they had been dying at his feet.

He readied his claws.

Golden light shot down over him and Lucifer raised his arms, shielding his face as he diverted course, flying backwards to evade the scorching beam. He clenched his jaw as his skin peeled and clothes burned away, the combined scent filling the air.

"Lucifer."

He broke free of the light, twisted towards her and dropped hard, his wings faltering as his shadows dissipated.

Nina shoved past the Hell's angels and ran towards him.

Lucifer hit the pavement with such force that he shook the ground of Hell, causing her to stumble. She refused to fall though, her arms flailing at her sides as she struggled for balance and kept running towards him. He willed her to go back as he tried to push himself up and fought to bring his shadows back as his body raced to heal the burns that covered him.

She shook her head, tears spilling onto her cheeks, as if she had heard him and refused to obey.

He growled a curse and pushed his palms against the splintered black flagstones. His hands had already repaired themselves, leaving perfect white skin and long black talons behind. He gritted his teeth and mustered his strength, calling on every last shred of it to fuel his healing ability. Smooth skin raced up his arms and he could feel it moving up his legs, but he feared it wouldn't be quick enough.

He could feel Mihail behind him, could sense the angel approaching him, and knew without looking that the male was coming to strike him down while he was weakened.

His Hell's angels took off, powerful red wings beating the air as they went after the remaining guardian angels. He would be mad at them for going against his orders later. Right now, he needed all the time he could get in order to gather the strength to fight.

Shadows fluttered from Lucifer's bare shoulders, giving him a sliver of hope that felt like torture, because at the same time despair burned in his heart.

Despair that grew with each step closer Mihail came.

Lucifer managed to turn towards him, grunting as white-hot fire burned in his bones and the scent of blood filled the air, his blackened flesh splitting open in places. Around him, flashes of light told him that his men had done their work, sending the remaining guardian angels back to Heaven.

Leaving only Mihail.

Mihail raised his flaming blade and cut through the air with it.

An arc of golden light formed and shot towards Lucifer.

It seemed it ended here.

Just when he had found a reason to live again, a reason to strive to be a better man and rise onto his feet once more, casting aside his need for vengeance and embracing the light that flickered within his heart.

Nina.

His eyes widened as she appeared in front of him, standing in the path of the blast.

Shielding him.

"No!" Lucifer tried to kick off towards her, reaching for her with both hands in order to grab her and teleport her to safety with the last of his strength, but his leg gave out and he hit the ground hard.

The arc of light reached her.

Black shadows exploded outwards from her, engulfing both her and him and tearing through the light, driving it back. They streamed around him in all directions, lashing at the remaining spires of the courtyard and sending Mihail flying through the air.

Lucifer stared in disbelief.

He knew Nina was pregnant without a doubt now, because Mihail had come for her, and the baby would attempt to protect her from harm as it viewed her as a vessel, something vital to its survival, but it was no more than a fertilised egg at present.

It wasn't possible the baby was already sentient and aware of the danger its mother had been in.

A tsk sounded behind him.

"I thought I warned you about messing with my family?" Erin stepped around Lucifer, her red eyes locked on Mihail.

Lucifer couldn't quite believe it.

His daughter had come to help him.

His daughter had openly called him family.

He stared at her and she glanced down at him, winked, and then grimaced and covered her eyes.

"Would you put something on?" She shuddered and turned away, fixing her attention back on Mihail.

Lucifer looked down at himself. Perfect healed pale skin. Every inch of it exposed.

He closed his eyes, drew down a deep breath and did something he hadn't done for a very long time indeed.

He called his armour.

The violet-edged obsidian breastplate covered his upper torso, the pointed strips of metal materialised over his hips and his black loincloth, and greaves appeared around his shins with his black leather boots. He sat back on his heels as his vambraces enclosed his forearms, each bearing a rampant dragon on them.

Crimson and gold eyes looked down at him, curiosity burning in them together with a desire to mention that he had the same armour as two other angels. Asmodeus, his creation, and the fallen angel, Nevar.

Lucifer glared at the owner of those eyes, daring the immense Hell's angel to say a word about it.

The large red-haired male merely grinned at him, and Lucifer knew he had stored it away for use at a later date.

He was about to make sure the wretched maggot never spoke of it, even though he knew that killing Veiron would only get him into trouble with his daughter, when Veiron shifted towards him.

It was then Lucifer noticed the squirming bundle in his thickly-muscled arms, pressed against the soft material of his black t-shirt.

Dante.

The thought of his grandson in danger was the last straw. Darkness washed through him again and his wings tore from his back, his horns flared from behind his pointed ears and he staggered onto his feet.

Mihail would never touch his family.

He lumbered forwards, slowly gaining strength with each step. Nina turned towards him and was moving the second her eyes fell on him. His heart warmed, filled with light at the way she looked at him with love and concern in her eyes despite his demonic appearance.

Just as she reached Lucifer, Dante erupted in a fit of giggles, stealing her focus.

She stared at the little boy as Veiron bounced him in his arms, a stunned expression settling on her beautiful face. Lucifer knew what she was thinking without needing to probe her mind. She was shocked to not only see an infant on the battlefield, but hear him laughing as if they were having a picnic, not a fight for their lives.

In time, she would come to understand Dante's ways.

The boy had no fear of battles.

If anyone dared to attempt to harm him, Dante's shadows would instinctively destroy them.

He was more powerful than both Lucifer and his mother right now, but it would change as he grew older, becoming aware of the world around him and learning other ways to protect himself.

Erin planted her hands on her hips and faced Mihail.

"You mess with my pops, and you're messing with me too." She glared at the angel as he picked himself up. "Whatever fucked up plan Heaven has, they can shelve it. Dante will never be my father's vessel. Nina's baby will never be your pawn. And I'm not a power in the mortal realm or some bullshit excuse for you to hurt Nina and mess around with her like this. If Heaven even so much as thinks about touching her, or the baby, you'll damn well discover where my allegiance lies."

Lucifer had to hand it to his daughter, she knew how to strike a bargain.

Erin looked back at him and smiled. "It lies with my family."

He cursed himself for being a sentimental fool, but her words touched him. He didn't deserve her after everything he had put her through, and he didn't deserve Nina, but both were a balm that were healing his wounds and making him whole again.

The light that Erin had brought to life in him, Nina had made blossom, until it and the darkness held sway over equal measures of his soul.

Lucifer knew he would never be good again, that his sins were still blemishes on his soul that he would bear for eternity together with his duties as the ruler of Hell, but he could still be a good man for those who were dear to him.

For those who loved him for who he was now and would never betray him.

Mihail readied his sword.

Lucifer threw his hand forwards and the male grunted, his expression tightening as he fought the wave of power Lucifer sent at him. He increased the pressure on the angel, scowling at him as the male fought back and struggled to remain on his feet. Lucifer growled, the darkness within him growing again as he thought about everything the angel had done to Nina.

Sweat broke out on the male's brow, his face reddening as his legs trembled.

They buckled beneath him and he hit the cracked black pavement hard, his breath leaving him in a rush.

Victory belonged to Lucifer.

The darker part of himself said to deal the final blow and remove Mihail from his life forever.

Nina shifted, drawing his focus back to her. She looked between him and the angel, a touch of concern and wariness in her eyes.

Lucifer huffed.

Looked at Mihail.

A few days ago, he wouldn't have hesitated. He would have destroyed Mihail. Now, he found he couldn't do it. Now, when he looked at Mihail, he saw the man he had been millennia ago, and the light inside him said to ensure that what had happened to him didn't happen to the angel.

"Do not blindly follow orders, Mihail. Sometimes it is not the best course of action, no matter how much loyalty you feel." Lucifer lowered his hand to his side and glared at the angel when the male's icy eyes widened. "Do not think I will not kill you if you ever dare to come near me or my family again. I will not let you have Nina, but I will not fight you either. We have a common enemy now. Our powers are best expended fighting the princes of Hell."

The shock in Mihail's eyes only grew and Lucifer raised his hand again before the angel could voice the words he could see running through his tiny mind, questioning whether he meant they were now allies in a battle to protect the mortal realm.

"You are banished from this realm. Do not set foot in it again." Lucifer flicked his fingers towards Mihail and the angel disappeared.

Leaving him with just three people looking at him through shocked eyes.

He glared at each of them in turn.

None of their expressions changed so he growled for good measure.

Nina actually smiled at him.

He huffed at her, realising that he was always going to fail to intimidate her. She knew him too well and knew he wouldn't hurt her.

Erin grinned and jerked her thumb towards the place where Mihail had been. "Did you at least send him somewhere horrible?"

Lucifer cracked a smile. "The middle of the arctic ocean. There is nothing more irritating than wet feathers and freezing conditions."

Veiron grunted in agreement.

"Nice." The crimson in her eyes faded as she glanced at Veiron and Dante, her smile gaining warmth and losing its humour.

She took measured steps towards her husband and child, and embraced both of them. Dante squirmed and opened bright golden eyes, and reached for his mother.

Lucifer bit back a sigh at the tender sight of his daughter taking her child and cradling him, her gaze soft as she peered down at him.

Coming to know his daughter had made Lucifer miss knowing of her when she had been a baby. He had come to realise that he would have enjoyed being there for her, raising her and watching her grow into an incredible woman, and that perhaps he would have been set on his path towards the light long before now.

He might have become a man more deserving of Nina's love.

Love that part of him still feared he would never have.

He lowered his gaze to Dante as Erin rocked him. He had missed his daughter's childhood, but he was determined to be there for Dante as the boy grew up. His intentions hadn't been noble when he had brought Erin and Veiron together, had awakened her powers and set her on the path towards having Dante. He had desired the boy as his vessel, but that desire had disappeared the moment he had set eyes on Dante.

He could never bring himself to corrupt the boy.

His golden gaze slid towards Nina where she stood just feet from him, her green eyes filled with tenderness as she watched Erin with her son.

She was pregnant.

His child grew inside her and that flooded his heart with warmth and light, filled him with emotions he would have considered a weakness just days ago.

Before he had met her.

Now, he didn't want to extinguish those emotions. He wanted to embrace them.

He would ensure Nina survived the birth of their child, and he would give that child everything they desired. He would do his best to raise it well with her, because now he felt capable of doing such a thing.

Now he knew how to cherish rather than corrupt.

Dante reached for Nina. Erin looked to her and back down at Dante. The boy stared up at his mother and she nodded, as if she had sensed something from him and was responding to it. She turned with Dante, carried him over to Nina and held him out to her.

Nina's peridot eyes darted between the boy and Erin, her uncertainty making Lucifer's feet move, carrying him towards her so he could offer the comfort that she needed. When he reached her, she glanced at him, and then down at the boy again. She pulled down a breath and very carefully reached for Dante, taking him into her hands and lifting him.

Dante giggled and pressed chubby hands to her cheeks.

Erin smiled. Veiron smiled too.

Lucifer had the feeling he was missing something, and he didn't like it.

"Explain," he snapped and Erin raised a single eyebrow at him.

Then grinned.

"Around the time someone went invasion of the body snatchers on me, Dante learned to use telepathy." Erin glanced back down at her son, her eyes shining with love and amusement. "He wanted to hear my voice. He hasn't been able to switch it off since then… so we've kinda been subjected to a constant stream of baby babble most of the time and I can't tell you how annoying that is."

She glared at Lucifer.

He refused to apologise for what he had done. It had been necessary.

"You can understand him sometimes though?" he said and Erin nodded.

"Sometimes he gets his words straight and makes some sense." She tickled Dante's chin and he bounced in Nina's arms, making her eyes shoot wide and her grip on him tighten as fear flashed across her pretty face.

"What did he say?" Lucifer peered closer at the boy, wondering whether they would be able to communicate telepathically soon. It was bad enough when Erin accidentally invaded his mind. He wasn't sure he was ready to deal with 'baby babble' as Erin had put it.

Erin smiled over Dante's head at him. "He wants to know when he gets to meet his aunt."

It took Lucifer a moment to make sense of that. When he did, he groaned and scrubbed a hand down his face, and tried to ignore the sympathetic look Veiron gave him.

"Another daughter? One is trouble enough." Lucifer grinned inwardly when Erin huffed and scowled at him. "I had hoped for a son."

"A daughter?" Nina beamed, and she was radiant and breathtakingly beautiful, making him instantly change his mind.

Daughter. Son. Triplets. He didn't care. Not when she looked so happy.

He could raise a whole army of hellions with her if she kept smiling at him like that, overflowing with love and joy.

Her smile faltered and he reached for her, placing his hand on her shoulder as he sensed the reason for her sudden change in feelings.

"I will find a way to ensure you survive the birth, Nina. I swear it. I will not lose you."

She nodded, but the solemn edge to her eyes didn't lift.

Erin clapped a hand down on her shoulder, making her jump and suddenly tug Dante to her, swiftly cradling him to her chest. Lucifer curled his arm around the boy too, ensuring she didn't drop him and hoping to allay her fears that she might.

"Don't worry," Erin said and when her words didn't have the desired effect on Nina, she pouted. "I said, don't worry."

"Why not?" Nina asked and Lucifer had been close to asking that question too.

His daughter had something else up her sleeve. He could tell by the mischievous look in her eyes, the one that told him she was enjoying herself because she had some power over him for a change.

Erin stroked Dante's head, sweeping his black hair to one side and neatening it. The boy gurgled and kicked in response, wriggling in Nina's arms. Lucifer looked down at Dante and then at Nina, heat spreading through his chest at the sight of her with the boy. He couldn't help imagining that it was their child in her arms.

She would make a wonderful mother.

There was so much love in her.

Erin slid him a knowing look. Lucifer schooled his features, hiding his feelings from his daughter. The wicked edge to her smile said it was too late for him. He was done for. She knew how deeply he loved the woman he held in his arms and the thought of having a child with her, and he was never going to hear the end of it.

"Dante can protect people from harm," Erin said and stroked Dante's pink cheek. "He protects Veiron and me, and anyone he feels like protecting really... and he feels like protecting you. When the times comes, we'll bring Dante to you and he'll be able to protect you from the power of your baby."

Nina raised her eyes to meet Lucifer's, and he could see that she needed to hear it from him.

He hadn't thought about it as a method of keeping her safe, because he hadn't believed Erin would do such a thing for him, allowing her son to help him, but his daughter was right.

"Erin is telling the truth. Dante has the power to protect others from harm, Nina." Lucifer lowered his hand and gently stroked the small of her back. "Even powerful angels cannot exert their power on those he chooses to protect. It may mean that I also still possess that protective power and that it was not stripped from me when I fell. I have not tried to protect people, not before today, but it is possible that I could help you withstand the effects of giving birth."

"And Dante too." Erin took Dante from Nina. "Because I'm not missing the birth of my half-sister… mainly because I want to see my dear old dad lose his shit."

She grinned at him.

Lucifer scowled.

Nina laughed. "He really lost his shi—should we be swearing in front of Dante?"

Erin shrugged at the same time as Veiron.

"He can already swear in the demon tongue," Veiron said, his deep voice gruff but edged with affection as he looked at his son. "We think it came built in."

"Well, Lucifer certainly lost his temper a moment ago with the angels," Nina said, her smile holding and her words fuelling his hope and keeping it strong.

He had lost his temper, had revealed the darker side of himself to her, and she wasn't running from him.

Erin smiled. Veiron gawped at him.

"Your name is Lu—" he started.

"Silence, Maggot." Lucifer waved his hand and cut him off, stealing his voice from him. The immense male's lips moved but no sound left them.

He bared his fangs at Lucifer, his eyes turning crimson again as his red wings unfurled from his back and his black clothing melted away, replaced by the pieces of his scarlet and black armour.

Erin sighed, stepped up to her husband and pressed a kiss to his right biceps. That single brush of her lips seemed to work magic on the male, easing his anger so his eyes darkened back to their natural colour.

"I think I've tried his patience enough for one day," Erin said and rested her cheek on Veiron's arm. She glanced up at him. "Speak, Baby. Get it off your chest and let's get out of here."

Veiron reached down, covered Dante's ears, and snarled at Lucifer, "Little Fucker."

Charming.

Lucifer waved him away, and the male looked as if he wanted to land a physical blow on him rather than the verbal one he had been allowed to deal.

"You really owe me now, Pops." Erin pressed closer to Veiron and darkness flared, engulfing them both. When it dissipated, they were gone.

Nina's gaze burned into the side of his face.

Lucifer slowly edged his eyes towards her.

He had a feeling that he would be paying his daughter back for a long time to come.

But he also had a feeling it would be worth it.

Because she had given him a chance with Nina.

A shot at winning her heart.

CHAPTER 16

Nina wasn't sure she would ever get used to teleporting. The second her feet touched the black stone floor in her apartment in Lucifer's castle, her knees gave out. He caught her waist, his grip firm but gentle, as if he feared hurting her.

She wasn't sure he could ever do that.

He seemed incapable of it.

He attempted to prove her wrong by releasing her and drawing away from her, distancing himself as he backed towards the fireplace across the room. His striking golden eyes touched on everything but her, refusing to settle on her even when she moved towards him. He had been quiet from the moment his daughter and grandson had left with the big man she presumed was married to Erin.

A man who appeared to be an angel of Hell.

Seeing them together, seeing how deeply the man loved Erin and his son, and how much Erin clearly loved him back, had given Nina the final piece of courage she needed to face her feelings for Lucifer.

"Lucifer?"

He still refused to look at her, and she didn't like the troubled edge to his eyes. She wanted to take away whatever was bothering him, but she couldn't do that if he kept avoiding her gaze and remained silent.

"What are you thinking?" she whispered and closed the distance between them.

He tried to back away, but his bottom hit the rear of the red couch, stopping his progress.

Nina slowly approached him, afraid he would teleport away from her if she made him feel she was pushing him. She didn't want him to leave, and she didn't want to upset him. She wanted him to stay.

She wanted to make him feel better.

Whatever he feared, she would chase it away for him.

She would take care of him.

He lowered his head, his tousled black hair falling down to caress his brow. His horns were still out, and his wings brushed the back of the couch at his sides, but his skin was more cream than white and his lips were pink again.

She had expected to be afraid when she had seen him change, but no matter how long she had waited, that emotion hadn't washed over her. She hadn't feared him.

She had only feared for him.

He had disappeared on her after announcing that Mihail had come and her heart had lurched in her chest, fear filling it as she had realised he had gone to fight the angel again.

He had gone out to protect her.

The need to protect him had been so strong that she had sprinted through the building and burst out onto the battlefield without thinking through what she was doing, determined to make Mihail and the angels see that she didn't want to go with them.

She had reacted on instinct when she had seen Lucifer falling, burned from the weird light that had speared Hell. Everything in her had screamed at her to shield him, because she had felt certain that Mihail wouldn't dare hurt her. She was important to Heaven, and she had wanted to use that to her advantage in order to save the man she loved.

"Lucifer?" Nina placed her hand on the hard black breastplate that protected his chest, wishing she could reach through it to the spot between his pectorals, directly over his heart. "Tell me what you're thinking."

He closed his eyes and sighed, shifting the breastplate and her hand with it.

"Can you imagine what demons do to angels when they end up in Hell?" He slowly opened his eyes and lifted them, hesitating on her lips before he forced them up to meet her eyes.

The haunted quality to them told her the answer to that question and she placed her other hand against his cheek, unable to ignore her need to comfort him. He had been an angel once, and he had been cast into Hell. He wasn't asking her to imagine what demons did to angels in his realm now, while he ruled, because she had seen angels in this land, both his men and those of Heaven, and they had been left alone by the demons.

He was asking her to picture what it had been like for him.

He looked off to his right. "It was a land without a ruler then. Nothing to stop them or hold them back."

"They did terrible things to you, didn't they?" Her palm trembled against his cheek, her heart aching as she pictured his back and all the scars that littered it.

I have survived atrocities. Torture so vile.

His words haunted her and her mind ran with them, throwing image after image at her, each worse than the last. How many times had he been tortured?

She stared at his chest, remembering how he had reacted when she had touched the vertical ridges of scar tissue on his back.

How many times had they torn his wings from him?

Tears lined her lashes and she blinked them away, not wanting him to think that she pitied him because she knew it would upset him. It wasn't pity that filled her heart. It was anger. Fury. Rage that he had been put through so much pain.

Nina pressed her palm to his cheek and drew his gaze back to her. "You were betrayed."

His eyes searched hers and he tried to look away again but she refused to let him.

His gaze narrowed, darkening a degree. "I gave them my loyalty… I carried out my orders without question… and in return I was cast into this hell. I am not a good male, Nina. I did not choose the right path, even though I tried to walk it. I did not have the strength to remain walking towards the light as you did."

He disappeared and she feared he had left her, but then he spoke from behind her and she turned to face him.

"I trod the darker path… I allowed that darkness into my heart and I embraced it. Whatever torment I had suffered, I dealt it back a hundredfold. I bathed Hell in the blood of my torturers." He held her gaze, his golden eyes turning crimson. "I destroyed what had been here, a prison for the angels who had sinned as I had, and in its place I built my own kingdom… a kingdom I rule, Nina… and nothing will change that."

Not even her.

She knew that.

She knew that if she chose Lucifer, she chose everything that came with him. She chose a life in Hell, with a man who had a duty to punish those who were sent to his realm, as he had been punished before them.

"We've both been punished for things that weren't our fault," she said and continued before he could speak. "But now we have each other."

He snarled and advanced a step, his enormous black wings unfurling to span the room.

She didn't flinch. Didn't move a muscle. She wasn't afraid of him. He could rage all he wanted, test her as much as he liked, but she would never turn her back on him.

Because he was her home.

He was where she belonged.

"We are not the same, Nina," he growled and stalked another step towards her, his horns flaring forwards as his ears turned pointed. "You are light and beauty… I am darkness and sin. I deal in pain and suffering. Everything that was dealt to me in this realm, I now deal to others."

Nina sighed softly. "That isn't truly the case is it?"

He glared at her, but there was a flicker of confusion in his red eyes, a pause in his step that told her that she could get through to him if she just kept pressing forwards and refused to retreat.

She could make him understand her feelings for him and that they were real.

He was lashing out at her because he thought they weren't a good fit, he thought that she would never accept the things he had done or the person he was, and that wasn't the case at all.

They weren't perfect, no couple was, but she loved him and she knew he loved her.

He had already told her as much, just without saying the actual words. He had shown her that he loved her.

She would show him that she loved him.

"You have angels working for you. I've seen them, remember?" She took a step towards him and he frowned at her feet and bared his fangs. Nina ignored the warning and advanced another one. "Tell me that I'm wrong if I'm wrong… but when an angel is sent here now, they don't receive punishment, do they? You take them in. You give them a new home."

He tossed a black look at her, but he didn't deny her.

"They serve you and you're lenient on them… although, I imagine some get hit by the pointy end of your temper."

His face darkened and he growled through his fangs. Nina smiled at him. She was getting to know him now. He wouldn't hurt her. All he could do right now was growl, huff and attempt to scare her, and she found it amusing and endearing in a way. He wanted to be the monster he had painted himself as, the one she was meant to see him as because of all the stories people told about him, but all she could see was a man that loved her and was hurting because he feared she would leave.

"You don't punish the angels as you were punished." Another step.

He rose to his full height and glared down at her, his black wings stretched wide, spanning the room and fluttering like smoke.

"It does not change anything," he said, his tone gruff and dark.

Nina shook her head. "It changes everything. You changed everything. You said that yourself. You seized power and changed things here. You might have embraced the darkness, but it doesn't rule you, Lucifer. I've seen the good in you. You're not heartless."

His shoulders dipped and his handsome face softened, the red in his eyes fading.

"I am," he whispered, raised his hand towards her as his eyebrows furrowed and swept his fingers downwards through the air, as if stroking her cheek. "I was heartless from the moment I met you. You stole it from me."

Nina's lips curved into a soft smile and she stepped close enough to him that he could touch her cheek as he clearly needed to. He brushed his fingers across it as she continued walking, his head dipping to keep his eyes locked on hers.

She pressed her left hand to his black breastplate, tilted her head back and smiled up at him. "You have a heart."

He opened his mouth and she lifted her right hand and pressed her finger to his lips to silence him.

"You have my heart."

Warmth flooded his golden eyes and she heated inside, feeling light as he gathered her into his arms and pressed a kiss to her fingertip.

"You are not lying," he whispered against it and she was tempted to chastise him for still wanting to doubt her, but she let it go instead.

She could understand why he couldn't accept the heart she was offering him, her love and devotion, and that it was going to take him time to overcome the doubts that lived within him, born of his position and his past.

She would give him that time and she would make him understand. She would keep showing him that she loved him and wanted to be with him. She would show him every day that her feelings for him were true, until the day that he believed her, and beyond.

She would never stop showing him.

Nina slid her arms around his neck, locked her hands behind his head, and tiptoed as she lured him down to her.

She pressed her lips to his and he tensed, going still for a heartbeat before he responded. He curled his arms around her back, grabbed her bottom, and raised her up him. His mouth claimed hers, the ferocity of his kiss melting her and tearing a moan from her lips.

He pulled back from her, his golden eyes searching hers, flooded with hope and affection that brought a smile to her lips and only made her want to kiss him again.

She placed her hands against his cheeks, held his gaze, and lost herself in it.

She wasn't afraid of him or what she was doing. She felt certain that this was where she belonged, that this was her destiny, and that she would be happiest here. She wanted no part of Lucifer's duties, but she understood that he had to carry them out. He was part of the balance in the world.

A world that she was going to bring a child into with him.

It still sounded crazy to her.

But it was the best sort of crazy and she wouldn't change it.

"You're going to be a wonderful father," she whispered and his expression softened, bringing a smile back onto her lips.

He began to smile but it wavered, and a trace of fear entered his eyes. She shook her head but it didn't stop that fear from taking root and spreading. Nina smoothed her palms over his cheeks and stroked his black hair, needing to soothe him. She didn't want to think about what might happen. She wanted the next nine months with him to be heaven, not spent living in fear.

"You'll never let anything bad happen to me." She ran her fingers through his hair, sure of that in her heart.

Resolve vanquished the fear in his eyes. "And what makes you say that, Little Mortal?"

"Because you *like* me." Nina was beginning to think that meeting Erin had unleashed her playful side, the one that had been dormant for nearly a decade, because she couldn't stop teasing him now that she knew he responded to it so wonderfully.

He stared at her in silence. "Like?"

She nodded. He frowned and turned with her, carrying her towards the four-poster bed.

"I do not think like is the right word." A flicker of mischief shone in his eyes and she had to force herself not to smile as the heavy air in the room lifted, becoming lighter and warmer with each step he took and each inch further he relaxed.

"Oh, it isn't?" She wrinkled her nose up and wrapped her legs around his waist. "Adore then. You adore me."

He shook his head, set one knee down on the bed and laid her down on it. He braced his hands on either side of her shoulders, his gaze tender as he looked down at her.

"I believe the word you are looking for is love." He went to dip his head to kiss her.

Nina pressed her palms to his chest. "Love?"

He nodded, his golden eyes sincere and filled with that emotion. "I love you."

It was her turn to stare at him. She hadn't actually thought he would come out and say it.

He grinned wickedly, dropped his head and kissed her hard.

Nina moaned into his mouth, arched her body up to press into his, and pulled him down against her. He groaned and rolled with her, bringing her up on top of him, and her eyes widened as cool air washed over her.

She was naked.

She pressed her hands to his chest.

His bare chest.

Heat spread through her, turning her blood to fire as only he could and making her burn for him. She had the feeling that there were some powers he had that she would come to love.

The ability to make clothing disappear being top of that list.

Nina looked down at the man beneath her, not seeing an evil being at the centre of a thousand tales of terror, but seeing a man who had just laid his heart on the line and made himself vulnerable, exposing the softest parts of himself with his confession. He had braved rejection, had stripped himself bare for her, and now she would show him that he had no reason to fear, because she loved him deeply too.

All of him.

She raised her hands from his chest, reaching towards his handsome face. His golden eyes tracked her every move, and he tensed when she didn't stop to caress his cheeks, instead choosing to skim her fingers across the tips of the shiny obsidian horns that curled from his tousled black hair. He closed his eyes and tried to turn away, attempting to shun her touch, and she made a noise of disapproval in her throat.

His eyes flicked open, sliding towards her and narrowing as they did so, but they held only confusion, not any irritation that she had reprimanded him, a powerful and dangerous man.

"Don't pull away from me, Lucifer," she whispered and his gaze softened and warmed, his body relaxing beneath hers, and she again felt she held power over him whenever she uttered his name.

She would whisper it a thousand times over into the shell of his ear, against the smooth column of his throat, and across his hard chest if it would make him listen to her and believe that she loved him. She wanted to capture and captivate him just as he had her.

She wanted him to know that he truly held her heart in his hands now, and forever.

Nina pressed her fingers to his horns and angled his head back towards her. He didn't resist this time, and she thanked him with a tender smile. She stroked the curves of his horns and he shuddered beneath her, a groan leaving his lips as they parted and he tilted his head back, pressing it into the dark covers.

His hands claimed her hips, short black claws pressing into her flesh, and his eyes slipped shut.

"Nina," he murmured, voice thick with tension but edged with passion, hunger that she could feel the evidence of pressing against her slick core.

She ground against his rock hard length, ripping a feral grunt from him and making him dig his claws in deeper.

"You're beautiful," she whispered and he frowned and looked at her, his golden gaze questioning her sanity. She giggled and skimmed her hands down his horns, and his eyebrows furrowed as he sank his short fangs into his lower lip, every muscle on his torso tensing as he shuddered again. He liked that, and she planned to use it against him whenever she wanted to get her own way. "You are, Lucifer."

The one-two punch of stroking his horns and uttering his name seemed to be his undoing. He growled and rolled with her, so swiftly her head spun as she landed on her back on the mattress beneath him.

When the dizziness passed, she found herself staring up at a very different male.

Black shadow wings fluttered from his shoulders, shutting out the rest of the room and keeping her focus locked on him.

As if she could focus on anything else when he was wedged between her bare thighs, his hard cock pressing against her aching centre.

She would have rubbed herself against it to alleviate that ache if he hadn't looked so damn serious again.

His horns had flared forwards, reminding her of a bull, and the tips of his ears were pointed. The gold in his eyes was gone, crimson burning fiercely in its place. The intensity of his gaze pinned her as effectively as the delicious weight of his body.

He was testing her.

She wouldn't fail, because she didn't see a monster above her, as he wanted her to. She only saw Lucifer.

She saw the man she loved with all of her heart.

Nina raised her hands, fearlessly lifting them towards his face and not hesitating, not even when his skin paled, and his lips darkened towards black and peeled off twin rows of sharp teeth.

She sighed and brushed her fingers across his sculpted cheeks, ignoring his snarl as she stroked his pale skin.

"You don't frighten me, Lucifer," she murmured softly and wrapped her legs around his waist, pressing the heels of her feet into his bare backside and locking him in place against her. "I'm not going to run away... I'm staying right here... can't you see that?"

He didn't look as if he could.

Nina's heart ached for him.

She cupped his cheeks, brushing the lobes of his pointed ears, and slowly drew him down towards her as she searched his eyes, hoping he would see the truth in hers and believe what she was about to say.

"Can't you see that I love you?"

Gold shot through the crimson in his eyes as they widened.

She opened her mouth to tell him again that she loved him, to say it over and over until he believed her and believed that someone in this world could love him, that he deserved every drop of the affection she felt for him.

He swooped on it before she could get the first word out, swallowing it in a fierce kiss that set her on fire.

Nina instantly responded, tugging him closer to her as she kissed him with all the passion and affection she felt for him. His sharp teeth grazed her tongue, making her flinch, and then gasp in surprise when they were suddenly smooth and straight again. He had changed them for her, because she was right about him.

He could never hurt her.

She moaned as she angled her head and deepened the kiss, losing herself in it as Lucifer gathered her into his arms, shifting his hands beneath her shoulders before curling his fingers over them to lock her in place against him.

He groaned and nibbled her lip before kissing down her jaw. She tilted her head, leading him towards her throat, and sighed as he skimmed his lips down it, pausing briefly to nip at her flesh and send a thousand volts shooting down her body. Her nipples tightened and her belly heated, aching with a need to feel him inside her, completing her again. She rocked against him, trying to gain a glimmer of satisfaction.

Lucifer swept his mouth down over her collarbone, his body sliding lower between her legs as he moved, and she huffed as the hot hard length she had been enjoying rubbing against was stolen away from her.

She wanted it back.

She curled her hands around his horns and he groaned against her breast before wrapping his lips around her left nipple and sucking it into his mouth, hard enough to rip a gasp from her. Tingles shot out in all directions as he suckled, spearing her belly and stoking the inferno there. She whimpered and writhed beneath him, silently begging him to give her some relief.

When he refused to move, she pressed down on his horns, pushing him towards where she needed him.

He lifted his head and narrowed his golden eyes on her, a sultry and seductive edge to his gaze that thrilled her.

Nina bit her lip and kept pressing him downwards, guiding him. The more she forced him, the darker his gaze grew, the hunger in it spiraling to match the ferocity of the one living inside her. He liked her commanding him.

She shoved harder.

Lucifer snarled, grabbed her hips in a bruising grip, and pushed her up the bed with such force that she gasped. An electric thrill shot through her and she wanted to push him again, craved the feel of him using his strength on her, dominating her and taking command.

He did just that as he dropped his head, spearing her folds with his tongue as his fingers clutched her hips, pressing in so hard she felt sure she would have bruises come the morning.

She didn't care.

The feel of his tongue stroking over her nub, flicking and laving it, was worth any bruises she might pick up.

She moaned and arched her back, raising herself against his face, seeking more from his wicked tongue. He groaned against her and shifted his hands, grasping her bottom and holding her off the bed as he tormented her. Each deep hard stroke of his tongue took her higher, teasing her until she felt as if she was floating but at the same time it was torture. She needed more. It wasn't enough.

She pressed her heels into the mattress and rocked against his face as she threw her hands above her head and clutched the pillows, twisting them in her fists. Moan after moan left her lips but he refused to give her what she needed.

"Lucifer," she whispered breathlessly.

He groaned and dropped lower, and the feel of his cool horns pressing into her thighs sent a stronger bolt of electricity through her, thrilling her and pushing her closer to the edge. He teased her entrance with his tongue, his horns wedging her thighs apart, and then lapped at her pert nub again, circling it before suckling lightly, causing a thousand tiny shivers to cascade through her. He shifted one hand, feathering his fingers down her folds, and her breath caught, anticipation ratcheting up to an unbearable degree as he stroked and caressed, circled her slick entrance but refused to press inside. She screwed her face up, the agonising wait making her restless and hungry, filled with a fierce need to feel him inside her.

She wriggled her hips, tried to catch his finger, to make him enter her, but he evaded her each time she was close.

She couldn't take it.

"Please," she murmured and released the pillows and reached for him. She needed more from him than teasing, craved the feel of him inside her, filling her up, being one with her, both of them lost in their passion. "I need you, Lucifer."

He lifted his head and she managed to open her eyes and look down the length of her body at him.

His golden eyes challenged her to say that again.

"I need you," she said, holding his gaze, and opened her arms to him. "I love you."

He growled, flashing fangs, and covered her with his body, driving into her in one hard deep thrust as his mouth claimed hers.

Nina cried into it as his rigid length filled her, stretching her and satisfying her ache to feel him inside her again.

She kissed him as he withdrew and plunged back into her, wrapped her arms around his neck and held on to him. When he tried to slow his frantic pace, she deepened the kiss and twined her legs around him, driving him on. She didn't want slow. Not this time. She wanted to feel him, feel his passion and need, and know it matched her own. She wanted to show him that they could let go and love each other, with nothing held back.

He grunted and flexed his hips, tearing a moan from her as he thrust deeper inside her before withdrawing almost all the way out of her. Each long stroke of his cock drove her higher, sending her out of her mind with a need to reach the precipice with him and tumble into a hazy abyss of bliss together.

She ploughed the fingers of her right hand through his hair, clinging to him as he drove into her, relentless and wild. Her left hand skimmed across his shoulder, short nails pressing in briefly as he struck deep inside her, pulling a cry of pleasure from her lips. She fumbled, looking for something to grasp and anchor her to him as he made love with her.

Nina grabbed the base of his wing.

Lucifer slammed forwards, driving hard into her, and arched upwards, throwing his head back as he roared.

The heat in her belly exploded, rushing through her, filling her blood with sparks that detonated in waves as her body quivered in time with his, quaking as bliss overcame her. His hard length throbbed, sending rippling aftershocks through her, heightening her pleasure. He breathed hard above her, his face screwed up, reflecting the ecstasy that filled every inch of her. His arms trembled, his body juddering as his climax rolled through him.

When his breathing levelled, he slowly opened his eyes and looked to his right, at her hand where it still grasped his wing, and then down at her, mild surprise written in the handsome lines of his face.

"I didn't realise they were so sensitive," she said, breathless as she struggled for air, marvelling at how fiercely he had reacted.

She had thought his horns were a trigger point for him, a method of getting her own way. The way he reacted whenever she touched them was nothing compared with how he had reacted when she had touched his wing.

She couldn't resist stroking her fingers along the soft arch of it to test her theory.

Lucifer shuddered, his face screwing up again, hips thrusting forwards to drive his softening length deeper into her. Yeah, he definitely had a thing for that. The moment she released him, he huffed and pinned her with a dark look she guessed was meant to be threatening.

"Do not think you have power over me, Little Mortal."

Nina smiled wickedly. "I don't think I have power over you, Lucifer."

She curled her hands around the nape of his neck and drew him down to her, capturing his lips in a soft kiss.

She whispered against his mouth, "I know I do."

He surprised her by chuckling and rolling with her, drawing her on top of him. "You will have to be patient with me, Nina. It has been a very long time since I had a master. I fear I will not submit to your rule easily or without a fight."

She pressed a kiss to his lips and stroked her fingers across his chest. "I don't want to rule you. I don't want to be your superior. I just want to stand by your side... and perhaps boss you around in the bedroom."

"That, I can live with. You will make me a fine queen."

Her eyes widened. She had never thought of herself as his queen, but she supposed if he ruled Hell as its king, she would become known as his lady and the occupants of the realm might view her as their queen. She wasn't sure she would ever get used to such a thing, and she didn't even want to think about it right now. She just wanted to be with Lucifer.

His hands slid down to the small of her back and he sighed against her lips.

Nina drew back and caught the flicker of concern surfacing in his eyes, and knew he was thinking about the future again, but in a different way to how she had been doing it.

She was thinking about growing used to living in Hell with him, and he was thinking about losing her.

"You'll never let anything happen to me, and I know that." She caressed his face and smiled down at him. "I'm not afraid, Lucifer. I know that we have a future together, and that it's going to be everything we ever wanted. I believe that in my heart. We'll get through this and we'll be a family."

"Family," he whispered, earnest desire in his voice that touched her. He wanted that, just as she did.

"Family… me, you and Lili."

Lucifer frowned. "Lili?"

She nodded and twined her fingers in his black hair. "Short for Lilith. I figured the daughter of the Devil needed a name suited to her parentage."

He smiled at last, rolled her onto her back and broke away from her. She was about to protest when he dipped his head and pressed his lips to her bare stomach.

"Lili," he whispered against it and stroked his fingers over it, making her wriggle as he tickled her. "You will be as beautiful as your mother, and as powerful as your father, and more loved than any other child in this world… my precious Lili."

He lifted his head and looked up at her.

"My precious Nina." He shifted up so he was eye-level with her again and rested his hand on her stomach as he looked down at her, his golden gaze filled with tenderness. "I will never let anything happen to you. I love you too much to lose you."

Tears lined her lashes, her heart filled to bursting in her chest. She had never felt so loved and needed, so cherished. "I know. I love you too, my precious Lucifer."

She lifted her head and kissed him as he wrapped his arms around her, clutching her to him in a way that said that now he had her he was never going to let her go. She held on to him, showing him that she wasn't going anywhere. She was staying right here with him.

Because he was her home.

And she knew that she was his.

Fate had made their paths cross and they walked a new one now, towards a future they both wanted with all of their hearts.

Together.

The End

Read on for a preview of the first book in the Her Angel: Bound Warriors romance series, Dark Angel!

DARK ANGEL

The images in the bright pool flickered past Apollyon's eyes at lightning speed but he could see them all, could bring each into focus and pause there a moment to understand what was happening in the scene before discarding it and allowing the flow to resume. It was a distraction he used daily, his every hour devoted to watching over the mortals.

In the long centuries he had studied the human world, he had seen a million or more changes, from the smallest accidental discovery to the grandest scheme that had altered the future of the race.

He had witnessed the growth of the mortals.

He had watched them forget his kind.

No one believed in angels anymore.

And his master had not called him forth from the bottomless pit in Hell in all the time he had been assigned to the dark realm of smoke and fire, hundreds of years passed choking on the stench of sulphur and bearing the presence of demons, and the king of Hell's vicious taunts that rang in his ears on a daily basis.

Yet Apollyon waited for the call to come, faithful and patient, committed to his duty even as others around him chose to live by their own commands. He had heard the tales from angels who had reason to enter Hell, whispers and rumours about how their fellow warriors had softened and fallen for mortal women, their devotion wavering and their commitment altering to their love.

He would do no such thing.

He had no interest in mortals.

His dark blue gaze darted around the silvery pool, following the history it was recording, stopping a moment on images that interested him.

Wars. Death. Bloodshed.

It was something that never changed. The one constant. Mortals seemed bent on destroying each other.

One day, his master would call him and Earth would know the true meaning of destruction.

The pool cast pale light on him and the jagged obsidian rocks that surrounded it, chasing back the bleak darkness of Hell.

He rolled his shoulders as he crouched near it with his elbows resting on his bare knees, his hands dangling in front of him. The intricate gold metalwork on the black greaves protecting his shins and the vambraces around his forearms caught the light and shone, reminding him of how it would reflect the sunlight when he flew.

A dull ache started behind his breastbone.

On a weary sigh, Apollyon stood and unfurled his black wings, unable to deny the need to feel air in his feathers.

The chest plate of his armour rode up his torso as he lifted his arms and stretched them too. He tilted his head back, another long sigh escaping him as he stared at the endless black ceiling of the cavern above him, a barrier that separated him from the sky he longed to fly in once again.

A sky he hadn't seen in too long.

If it hadn't been for the pool, he would have forgotten the blue of it, and the green of the grass and the trees, the bright colours of flowers. He would have forgotten the clear air and crystalline waters. He would no longer remember the breathtaking mountains and wide stretching plains.

He would only know the glowing gold of the fires that dotted the black cragged landscape that surrounded him, and the rivers of lava that snaked between onyx mountains and around the plateau he stood upon. He would only know the choking stench of the smoke that laced the air.

He would only know the darkness that swirled around him, as thick as oil in the air, a constant presence that he couldn't shake—could only bear.

Apollyon closed his eyes, shutting out Hell as he built a picture in his mind, formed an image that stirred a memory.

One where he had been flying, breathing fresh air and feeling it beat against him as the sun warmed his wings.

He heaved another sigh as the ache in his chest worsened, birthing a desire to soar above the cities again, unseen and unknown, and to speak with the angels who walked on Earth and watched over the mortals.

He longed to be free of the choking fires of Hell.

He forced himself to open his eyes and see the home that was his now, a place he couldn't escape without an order from his master.

A realm he despised.

He went to turn away from the torture of watching the world he couldn't experience and paused as his blue gaze caught on an image as it rippled across the silvery liquid.

He frowned and crouched again, the long strands of his black hair falling forwards to brush the skin exposed between the slats of his hip armour and his knees as he leaned forwards and stared at the image he had stopped before him.

A lone female.

It wasn't the first time he had seen her. Noticed her. The petite blonde liked to walk in the park alone these days and her expression was often troubled, as though she bore a heavy weight on her heart.

What was she thinking when she looked like that?

It was the first time he had wondered about a mortal, had found questions filling his mind as he watched and studied them rather than simply absorbing facts about the things he was seeing.

If he was feeling honest with himself, he would admit that the park wasn't the only place he had spotted her.

He had seen her indirectly too, picking her out of a crowd or glimpsing her passing through an image that had interested him, and each time his gaze had followed her until she had disappeared from view.

Now, she stood staring up at the Eiffel Tower and the clear blue sky beyond it, her back to him and the gentle breeze catching her short red dress and tousling her long fair hair. He didn't need to see her face to know that it was her.

No other mortal captivated him as she could.

Roses framed the view, obscuring much of her legs.

He cocked his head and ran his gaze over what he could see. He had never seen her dressed like this. She had always worn layers of clothing in the past, her legs covered and a thick black coat encasing her slender frame.

The seasons had passed so quickly and he hadn't noticed that it was summer where she was in Europe.

The image changed, panning up the height of the Eiffel Tower, and he wanted it to go back to her until he saw the stretching blue sky above the top of the tower.

Apollyon reached out to the pool, desperate to touch that sky and feel the sun beating down on his wings as he flew.

The image drifted away, replaced with a succession of others that he had no interest in as one thought spun through his mind.

It was summer.

He stood and imagined flying in that blue sky and how exhilarating it would be. He pictured the whole of Paris stretched out below him, the elegant stone buildings bright in the sunlight that would warm their dull grey roofs and the tree-lined avenues filled with mortals coming and going, enjoying the weather.

He had never been there but he knew it well from the images he had seen, had witnessed it grow from small simple buildings into a grand bustling city.

What would it be like to see such a place?

To see such a female in the flesh?

He shook that thought away. He had no interest in mortal women.

If he didn't, why did his heart stop whenever he saw her?

Apollyon looked back into the pool and then turned away from it. His duty was to his master. He had to remain here, guardian of the bottomless pit, suffering the acrid fires of Hell, until his master called him.

He chuckled mirthlessly at that.

No one was going to call him. He was going to spend the rest of eternity trapped in his own personal Hell.

A dark curse rolled off his tongue and a noise like thunder rumbled in the distance. A taunting voice echoed within it, attempting to fill his mind with poison. He shut the Devil out, refusing to succumb to the temptations he offered to all angels who entered his domain. He wasn't weak, an angel easy to sway. He was strong, easily pushed back against the Devil because he had been made to fight him.

As the wretch's voice faded, a sense that someone was speaking his name built inside him. He listened, trying to hear the voice of his master, sure that this time it wasn't the Devil provoking him because the feeling it evoked in him was different.

Familiar.

But no matter what he did, no matter how fiercely he strained, he couldn't discern where the call was coming from.

He could only feel it beating inside him, growing stronger by the second.

Tugging him upwards.

Apollyon grabbed his sword, buckled the sheath to his waist, and didn't wait for the call to come again. This was his chance to escape Hell and he would take it. He was finally being called. He had a mission again at last.

He spread his black wings and with a single strong beat lifted into the thick air. The wind from them blew the dark smoke back so it swirled beneath him as they raised him higher and higher, carrying him towards the ceiling of his prison.

He stretched a hand up to it.

The black rock parted before him.

He beat his wings harder, flying faster now as a streak of blue formed above him. Hundreds of feet of rock passed him in a blur and he could hardly breathe, struggled to contain the feelings colliding inside him as he exploded into the fresh air on the other side. He grinned and shot upwards, his black wings beating furiously against the warm air, and didn't stop until he reached the clouds.

Apollyon hovered there, casting his dark blue eyes over the world at his feet, the cooler air streaming through his long black hair.

It was as beautiful as he remembered, more so in fact.

The cities the mortals had built fascinated him, had him itching to see them with his own eyes at last, to experience what his fellow warriors could and see if everything lived up to the tales they had told him and the reports he had read.

But his mission came first.

Perhaps if he fulfilled it in a satisfactory manner, he would be allowed some freedom, could soak in the mortal world before he returned to his duties.

He swooped lower, searching for his mission and listening for his master's call.

What did he desire him to do?

Whatever it was, he would carry it out. He always did. He had destroyed many cities in his name and cast many sinners into the bottomless pit. He had fought the Devil and defeated him, keeping him contained in Hell. Whatever challenge his master presented, he would complete it.

He frowned when he saw the city stretched below him.

Paris.

The desire to go to the Eiffel Tower and find the mortal female was strong but he resisted it and flew over the city, seeking the source of the call and his mission.

The call was quieter now though, weaker than it had been in Hell, and he struggled to locate the source of it as he flew along streets and above avenues, invisible to mortal eyes.

It burned within him though, relentless and driving him to search, even when he was beginning to wonder if he would be searching forever and if this was just a cruel joke because he had cursed.

The Devil would do such a despicable thing. He had a strong voice and could throw it well, could have easily feigned retreat, making Apollyon think he had shut him out, only to trick him into thinking the other voice he had heard was a different one—that of his master.

The bastard had promised Apollyon that he would pay for all the times he had cast him back into Hell after all.

Was it possible this was a lie? A trick? Was it possible he had been so desperate to leave Hell that he had fallen foul of the Devil?

Apollyon swooped lower, effortlessly cutting through the warmer air, using the feel of it tickling his black feathers and washing over his skin to distract him from his troubling thoughts. Fears that were unfounded.

It wasn't the Devil who had lured him to Paris.

It wasn't.

Turning, he dived down a side street, skimming low above the heads of the mortals, causing a wind to gust against them. He smiled when they shrieked and grabbed their clothes to keep them in place. It was wrong to take such childish pleasure from doing such things, but all angels had a tendency to misuse their invisibility and he was sure it wouldn't be held against him by his superiors.

A strong beat of his wings and he was soaring upwards again, determined to find the source of the call that tugged at his chest.

He landed on the edge of the roof of an old pale stone building and looked across the city towards the Eiffel Tower. It speared the clear sky, surrounded by lush green at the base, a beacon that called to him as fiercely as the voice.

He pushed off in that direction and froze.

Someone was speaking his name again.

Apollyon focused, frowning as he scanned the city and tried to discern the direction it was coming from. His gaze shot back to the Eiffel Tower. There?

He ran to the far edge of the building and leaped off, waiting until he was close to the flagstones of the square below before he unfurled his wings and beat them, shooting straight across the square only a few feet above the ground. He ducked and weaved through the people and came out over a grassy bank. The river was ahead and beyond it the Eiffel Tower. He flew straight for it and then came to an abrupt halt in mid-air when he heard the call again.

It was behind him.

He scoured the people below. Was his master down there, amongst them, calling to him?

His master had several guises. Apollyon's eyes darted over the mortals, stopping for barely a second on each face. None of them matched how he remembered his master.

The call came more clearly this time, beating deep in his heart.

His gaze shot in the direction it had come from.

His eyes widened.

Her?

A fair-haired mortal female stood beside one of the fountains below, her back to him and the warm breeze playing with the short skirt of her dark red dress. The jets of water from the fountains sprayed high, the droplets catching the wind to reveal a rainbow and settling on his skin when it blew towards him.

Apollyon frowned.

It had to be the Devil's work.

He had been watching her, had cursed, and then she had called him.

It was ridiculous.

No mortal had the power to call an angel, and he had not had a different master since eternity began, although he didn't remember those days, had forgotten it all the first time he had been reborn and had only the recorded history in Heaven to go on.

Cautiously, Apollyon swooped down, closer to her, hovering barely twenty metres above her head.

Had she called him?

He needed to know, and he would find out.

He was going to speak to her for the first time.

DARK ANGEL

Centuries in Hell have taken their toll on Apollyon. Tired of guarding the Devil, he longs to break free of the dark realm. The trouble is, he can't leave without permission. When he feels someone calling him, he seizes his chance for freedom, but what awaits him in the mortal realm is the last thing he expects—the beautiful woman he has watched over from Hell, a witch who casts a spell on him and awakens the darkest desires of his heart.

Serenity is shocked when a wickedly sensual black-winged angel shows up in her city of Paris claiming that she summoned him when she was only casting a simple vengeance spell. He's no other than the angel of death! A very gorgeous, alluring angel of death who makes her feel she's in danger of getting her heart broken all over again.

When the lethally handsome warrior offers to obey her and give her revenge, Serenity can't resist the temptation, but can she resist the forbidden hungers the dark angel stirs in her?

Available now in ebook, print and audiobook

ABOUT THE AUTHOR

Felicity Heaton is a New York Times and USA Today best-selling author who writes passionate paranormal romance books. In her books she creates detailed worlds, twisting plots, mind-blowing action, intense emotion and heart-stopping romances with leading men that vary from dark deadly vampires to sexy shape-shifters and wicked werewolves, to sinful angels and hot demons!

If you're a fan of paranormal romance authors Lara Adrian, J R Ward, Sherrilyn Kenyon, Kresley Cole, Gena Showalter, Larissa Ione and Christine Feehan then you will enjoy her books too.

If you love your angels a little dark and wicked, her best-selling Her Angel romance series is for you. If you like strong, powerful, and dark vampires then try the Vampires Realm romance series or any of her stand alone vampire romance books. If you're looking for vampire romances that are sinful, passionate and erotic then try her London Vampires romance series. Or if you like hot-blooded alpha heroes who will let nothing stand in the way of them claiming their destined woman then try her Eternal Mates series. It's packed with sexy heroes in a world populated by elves, vampires, fae, demons, shifters, and more. If sexy Greek gods with incredible powers battling to save our world and their home in the Underworld are more your thing, then be sure to step into the world of Guardians of Hades.

If you have enjoyed this story, please take a moment to contact the author at **author@felicityheaton.com** or to post a review of the book online

Connect with Felicity:
Website – http://www.felicityheaton.com
Blog – http://www.felicityheaton.com/blog/
Twitter – http://twitter.com/felicityheaton
Facebook – http://www.facebook.com/felicityheaton
Goodreads – http://www.goodreads.com/felicityheaton
Mailing List – http://www.felicityheaton.com/newsletter.php

FIND OUT MORE ABOUT HER BOOKS AT:
http://www.felicityheaton.com

Made in United States
Troutdale, OR
06/19/2024

20675423R10108